The Thirtee

Natalie Sumner Lincoln

Alpha Editions

This edition published in 2023

ISBN : 9789357945387

Design and Setting By
Alpha Editions
www.alphaedis.com
Email - info@alphaedis.com

Contents

CHAPTER I
THE EVENTS OF A NIGHT

THE white-capped nurse dropped the curtains in place so that they completely shut out the night and equally prevented any ray of artificial light penetrating the outer darkness. Her eyes, blinded by her steadfast gaze into the whirling snow storm, were slow in adjusting themselves to the lamp lighted room and for some minutes she saw as in a blur the spare form of the physician standing by her patient's bed. Doctor Roberts turned at her approach and removed his finger from about the man's wrist. He met her glance with a negative shake of his head as he replaced his watch.

"Abbott!" he called softly, bending over the patient: "Rouse yourself and take some nourishment. You will never get your strength back if you don't eat."

Slowly, languidly Abbott's dark eyes opened and regarded the two figures by his bedside. They lingered in some curiosity on the trim figure of the trained nurse and then passed on to the physician.

"I'll eat later," he mumbled. "Leave me alone, now,"—and the heavy lids closed again over the eyes under which dark circles of pain testified to hours of suffering.

"Very well." Doctor Roberts spoke more crisply. "Miss Ward will be here to look after you. You must do what she says. I'll see you in the morning. Good night."

His remark met with no response, and picking up his bag Roberts started from the room. At the door he paused and motioned to Miss Ward to follow him. Stopping long enough to arrange Abbott's pillow in a more comfortable position, the nurse went into the hall, only to find that Doctor Roberts was halfway down the staircase. With a doubtful look behind her, Miss Ward ran lightly down into the lower hall which, lighted only by oil lamps, was long and rambling and used as a living room. Doctor Roberts walked over to a table and put down his bag.

"I am glad that you are here, Miss Ward," he began, courteously. "I feared the storm would detain you. You have not nursed for me before?"—with an inquisitive glance at the pretty woman before him.

"No, Doctor." Miss Ward's tapering fingers pressed out a crease in her starched gown. "This is my first case since my arrival in Washington."

"Oh! You are a graduate nurse?"

"Yes. I trained in New York." Her hazel eyes met his steadily. "They told me at the hospital of the urgency of this case and I took a taxi out here."

"Quite right. Add all your expenses to your bill," directed Roberts. "Paul Abbott has ample means. He should be in a hospital."

"But his condition, doctor."

Roberts nodded. "That is out of the question," he agreed, "*now*. Had his caretaker sent for me in time I would have had Mr. Abbott moved from this God-forsaken location to the city. As it is"—he pulled himself up short—"we must do the best we can ten miles from civilization." His smile vanished as quickly as it had come. "I am no lover of the country in the dead of winter. What time did you get here?"

"An hour ago. Have you any orders, doctor?"

"You can give him a dose of this through the night"—taking out a small phial and handing it to her—"the directions are on the bottle. It is essential that Mr. Abbott have sleep; if necessary, give him this by hypodermic." And he handed her two pellets.

"What stimulation do you wish me to use in case of sudden collapse?" Miss Ward asked as Roberts picked up his bag and walked toward the front door.

"Strychnine, twentieth of a grain," brusquely, as the hall clock chimed ten, but his hurried exit was checked by a further question.

"Has Mr. Abbott any family to be notified in case his condition becomes dangerous?" asked Miss Ward.

"No immediate relations." Doctor Roberts was manifestly impatient to be off. "There's a girl—Betty Carter—but I'm not sure that the engagement isn't broken. Good night." The high wind drove the snow, which had drifted up on the broad veranda, in whirling gusts through the front door and half blinded Roberts as he held it partly open. With a muttered oath he dashed outside to his automobile, parked under the shelter of the *porte cochère*.

Miss Ward heard the whir of the starting motor, the grinding of weed chains and the shifting of gears before she closed the outer vestibule door. It was with a sense of reluctance that she turned back into the silent house. The storm and her surroundings oppressed her.

The old homestead, turned from a large-sized, roomy farmhouse into a hunting lodge, with its wide entrance hall converted into a living room from which ran numerous twisting passages, was a gloomy place in winter. Through darkened doorways Miss Ward obtained a vague impression of larger rooms beyond which she judged to be library, dining room, and possibly a sunparlor.

Paul Mason Abbott, Senior, had prospered in his real estate business, and had acquired, in one of his deals, the country property, twenty miles from Washington, the National Capital, which, with a substantial fortune, he had bequeathed to his only son, Paul. The latter's career as a promising young architect had been interrupted by the World War. Paul had borne his share of the fighting, returning to his home with health shattered and a morbid desire to live alone.

He had closed his bachelor apartment in Washington in the early spring and spent the following months motoring about the country. Just before Christmas he had appeared unexpectedly at Abbott's Lodge and announced that he would reside there indefinitely. Corbin, the caretaker, had given him but a taciturn welcome, and neither he nor his wife had done more than provide Abbott with three meals a day and such heat as was absolutely necessary to warm the house.

Miriam Ward felt that even Corbin's presence, disagreeable as she had found the caretaker in her one interview with him upon her arrival, was preferable to the grotesque shadows made by the furniture as she hurried across the living room and up the staircase to her patient. Paul Abbott paid no attention to her as she moved about making her preparations for a long night's vigil.

Abbott's bedroom stretched across one wing of the house. Miss Ward was conscious of a touch of envy as she subconsciously took note of the lovely old pieces of mahogany with which the room was furnished—the highboy with its highly polished brass handles, the fine old bureau with its quaint mirror hanging above it; the antique desk in one corner and last, but not least, the carved four-post bedstead with its canopy and its long curtains. The handsome rugs on the floor deadened her footsteps as she moved about, and it was with a sense of shock that she heard the grandfather clock in the hall chime the hour of midnight. The sudden sound in the utter stillness aroused Paul Abbott as he seemed about to drop off to sleep and he lifted his head. Instantly Miss Ward was by his side, but he pushed away the glass of milk she offered him.

"Has she come?" he asked eagerly.

"She? Who?"

"Betty."

Miss Ward shook her head. Then observing his feverish condition more closely, she hastened to say soothingly: "She will probably be here as soon as the storm lets up."

Abbott looked at her appealingly. Thrusting his fingers inside the pocket of his pajamas he drew out a crumpled piece of paper.

"Betty wrote that she would be here to-night," he protested. "And you must let her in—you must—"

"Surely." Miss Ward again offered the rejected glass of milk. "Drink this," she coaxed, and obedient to the stronger will Abbott took a few swallows and then pushed the glass away. His head slipped back upon the pillow and Miss Ward deftly arranged the curtain of the four-poster so that it sheltered his eyes from the light of the wood fire burning on the hearth at the opposite end of the bedroom.

An hour later she was about to replenish the wood for the third time when a distant peal of a door bell caused her to drop the kindling with unexpected suddenness in the center of the hot ashes. As the sparks flew upward, she heard Abbott call out and turned toward the bed.

"It's Betty!" he exclaimed, with a feeble wave of his hand. "Go—go—let her in."

"I will, but don't excite yourself," she cautioned. "Lie down on your pillows, Mr. Abbott, and keep yourself covered," drawing the eiderdown quilt over his shoulders as she spoke.

Another, and more imperative peal of the bell caused her to hasten across the bedroom and into the hall. She peered ahead expectantly as she went down the staircase, hoping for a glimpse of the caretaker, Corbin. Evidently the bell had not disturbed his slumbers, for she could distinguish no one approaching in the semi-darkness. Unfamiliar as she was with her surroundings it took Miss Ward several minutes to let down the night latch and turn the old-fashioned key in the lock of the vestibule door. As she swung the latter open she was pushed back and two figures stepped across the threshold, closing the door behind them. The first, a tall slender girl, her handsome fur coat covered with snow, stopped halfway to the staircase and addressed Miss Ward.

"Where is Mr. Abbott?" she demanded. "And why have you kept us waiting so long?"

"I presume the caretaker is still asleep," replied the nurse. "Otherwise the door would have been opened more promptly. Mr. Abbott is ill in bed. Very ill," she added, meeting the girl's imperious glance with a steady gaze. "This is no hour for visitors for a sick man."

"Oh, the hour!" The girl turned disdainfully away. "I must see Mr. Abbott; it is imperative. You are the nurse?" with a questioning glance at her white uniform.

"Yes, and as such in charge of the sick room," crisply. "I cannot permit—"

"Just a moment," broke in the girl's companion, who, until that instant, had busied himself with closing both the vestibule and inner front door. As he stepped closer and unbuttoned his heavy overcoat Miss Ward caught a glimpse of his clerical dress. "This is Miss Elizabeth Carter, Mr. Abbott's fiancée, and I am Dr. Nash of Washington. Miss Carter received word that Mr. Abbott is alarmingly ill—"

"With small hope for his recovery." The words escaped Betty Carter through quivering lips, and looking closely at her, Miss Ward discovered her eyelashes wet with tears. "Don't keep us standing here when time is so precious," and turning she ran up the staircase, followed by the clergyman and Miss Ward.

An odd sound far down the corridor caused the nurse to hesitate before accompanying the others into the sick room, and for several seconds she stood poised outside the door, her head bent in a listening attitude. The sound, whatever it was, and Miss Ward could have sworn it was a faint whimper, was not repeated. She was thankful to turn from the contemplation of the dark, winding corridor to the companionship of her patient and his two belated visitors.

Dr. Nash had paused by the solitary lamp, but his efforts to induce it to burn more brightly resulted in extinguishing it entirely, leaving the bedroom illuminated by the firelight only. He turned at Miss Ward's approach and addressed her in a low voice.

"Get the lamp from downstairs," he whispered. "This one is burned out."

Betty Carter, paying no attention to the others, halted by the bedside just as Miss Ward started for the door.

"I've come, Paul," Miss Ward heard her say as she darted out of the room. "I am here to keep my word. Dr. Nash is with me."

Miss Ward's mystification lent wings to her feet, but when she made the turn of the last landing of the staircase her foot slipped on some snow left on the hardwood by the clergyman's rubbers, and she went headlong to the floor. Considerably shaken by her fall, it was some moments before she could pull herself together and get to her feet. Taking up the lamp with a hand not quite steady, she walked upstairs. As she entered the bedroom she saw Betty Carter standing apparently just where she had left her and Doctor Nash closing his prayerbook.

"... I pronounce you man and wife." The solemn words rang their meaning into Miss Ward's ears as she took in the significance of the scene. "Come, Betty, we have no time to linger," and stepping forward, Doctor Nash laid his hand on the girl's arm.

With a gesture as if awakening from a dream, Betty Carter raised her head and faced Miss Ward. The nurse almost cried out as she met the full gaze of her tragic eyes.

"Surely you are not going?" she exclaimed. "Now—after—?"

"Yes." Betty's beauty was of an unusual type and Miss Ward's heart gave a sympathetic throb as she came under the magnetism of her personality. "We—I will be back," and before Miss Ward could gasp out a question, she hurried swiftly from the room, the clergyman at her heels.

Her mind in a daze, Miss Ward stood in the doorway of the bedroom holding the lighted lamp so that they might see their way to the staircase, but her half-formed intention of carrying the lamp to the head of the stairs altered when she saw that the clergyman was provided with a powerful pocket searchlight. She stood where she was until she heard the front door close with a distinct slam, then went thoughtfully into the bedroom.

Placing the lamp on a small table by the side of the bed, she drew back the curtain of the four-poster and looked down at the sick man. He lay partly on one side, his eyes closed, and one hand tightly clenching the eiderdown quilt. For one long minute Miss Ward regarded him, her senses reeling.

The man lying in the bed was not her patient.

CHAPTER II
CAUGHT IN THE WEB

A LONG-DRAWN sigh cut the stillness. Slowly Miriam Ward raised her head and struggled to a more upright position. Her limbs felt stiff and cramped and she moved with difficulty. Without comprehension she watched a beam of light creep from underneath a window curtain and extend across the floor, its radiance widening as the sun rose higher in the heavens. The current of air from the opened window blowing indirectly upon her overcame her sense of suffocation, but her wild stare about the bedroom did not bring recollection in its train. The first thing to fix her attention was the fireplace and the darkened hearth—no heat was given out by the dead embers. Suddenly conscious of the chill atmosphere, she involuntarily grasped her dress and dragged it closer about her neck. The touch of the starched linen caused her to glance downward. She was wearing her uniform, therefore she was on duty!

Miriam Ward's dulled wits slowly adjusted themselves. She had reported for duty at the Registry; a call had come—from where? To attend whom? Roberts? No, that was the name of the physician. Ah, she had it—Paul Abbott. The chord of memory was touched at last and the events of the night crowded upon her. The man in the bed—

Stiffly Miriam scrambled to her feet and made a few halting steps to the bedside. It took all her will-power to pull aside the bed curtains and glance down. Paul Abbott lay partly turned upon his side, his fine profile outlined against the white pillowcase, and his right hand just showing outside the eiderdown quilt.

Miriam's hand tightened its grasp on the curtain and she leaned weakly against the side of the bed; but for its support her trembling knees would have given way under her. She had been the victim of a nightmare! The midnight visit of Betty Carter and the clergyman, the substitution of a stranger for her patient—all had been a hallucination conjured up by a too vivid imagination. She had slept on duty. That, in itself, was an unpardonable offense.

Raising her arm she glanced at her wrist watch—the hands registered a quarter past eight. Then nearly nine hours had passed and she had lain asleep. A wave of color suffused her white face and she grew hot and cold by turns. Her heart was beating with suffocating rapidity as she hurried to the windows and drew aside the long, heavy curtains and pulled up the Holland shades. The storm of the night before was over and the winter sunshine brought a touch of warmth to the room and a sense of comfort.

A glance at the fireplace convinced Miriam that it would require both time and fresh kindling wood to start a fire. It could wait until she had summoned the caretaker; the room was not so cold now that she had closed the window.

Retracing her footsteps she again paused by the bed and gazed at her patient. He still lay on his side, motionless. Miriam Ward caught her breath— motionless, aye, too motionless. A certain rigidity, a waxen pallor, indistinguishable in her first glimpse of him in the darkened room, held her eyes, trained to detect the slightest alteration in a patient's condition. Her hand sought his wrist, then his heart, then dropped limply to her side. Paul Abbott lay dead before her.

Her low cry was smothered in the bed curtain, which she pressed against her mouth, and for a moment she swayed dizzily upon her feet. Paul Abbott had died while she lay asleep within a few feet of his bed. Overwhelming remorse deadened every other feeling and held her spellbound. Fully five minutes elapsed before a sense of duty aroused her to action.

Wheeling around, Miriam staggered rather than walked to the telephone standing on Abbott's desk. She had jotted down Doctor Roberts' 'phone call the night before, but it took her several seconds to get the central at Washington, and still others passed before a man's voice told her that the physician was out making his morning rounds. At her urgent request the servant promised to locate Doctor Roberts and send him at once to Abbott's Lodge.

As Miriam replaced the receiver on its hook she was conscious of a feeling of deadly nausea and she stumbled as she walked across the room and into the hall. She must have aid. Her repeated calls brought no response. What had become of the caretaker and his wife? A noise of some one moving in the hall below caused her to run down the staircase to the lower landing.

"Here—here, this way!" she gasped, and saw vaguely outlined a woman's terrified face in front of her while the sound of a heavy tread coming down the staircase echoed in her ears. "Mr. Abbott—I—" Voice and strength failed her simultaneously, and before any one could reach her she lay in a crumpled heap on the landing, unconscious of the loud ringing of the gong over the front door.

It was approaching noon when a timid knock at her bedroom door brought Miriam Ward into the corridor and face to face with the caretaker's wife.

"If you please, Miss, the doctor says do you feel better?" The question came in a gasp, characteristic of Martha Corbin. A gray ghost of a woman, timid to the verge of cowardice, she seldom spoke unless addressed.

"Much better," replied the trained nurse. "Where is Doctor Roberts?"

"In there," with a jerk of her thumb over her shoulder. "He wants to see ye."

"Very well." Miriam Ward closed her bedroom door with a firm hand. She had regained some hold upon her composure as her attacks of nausea ceased and the throbbing in her head lessened. Doctor Roberts had left her two hours before with the admonition to remain in bed until he saw her again, but her anxiety of mind had prevented her following his directions. She paused involuntarily outside of Paul Abbott's bedroom, then, gathering courage, she stepped inside. Doctor Roberts turned at the sound of her approach and put down the telephone instrument.

"So you are up," he said gruffly. "Well, how are you? Feeling stronger?"

"Yes; thank you, Doctor." In spite of her determined effort to keep her voice expressionless, Miriam was conscious that it was not quite steady. "I—oh, Doctor, I don't know what to say." Her pent-up emotion was gaining the upper hand. "How to tell you—"

"What?" as she paused.

"That—that—I slept on duty."

Doctor Roberts eyed her steadily for what seemed an interminable minute. "So that was it," he remarked dryly. "Well, what then?"

The nurse's pallor was intensified, but her eyes did not falter in their direct gaze.

"I was asleep when Mr. Abbott died," she admitted, her hands clenching themselves in the pockets of her uniform.

Doctor Roberts' stare grew prolonged. "And this was your first case in Washington?" he asked, with marked emphasis.

"Yes." Miriam Ward moistened her dry lips with the tip of her tongue.

"Hardly a successful début," commented Roberts. His glance strayed beyond the nurse to a man standing in the shadow of a window curtain. "Give Miss Ward a chair, Alan."

Somewhat startled by the presence of a third person, Miriam accepted the proffered seat with relief; she was weaker than she had at first realized.

"Miss Ward," continued Doctor Roberts, "this is Mr. Alan Mason, of the Washington *Post*. He arrived here in time to carry you to your bedroom and then summoned me."

Miriam glanced upward and encountered the gaze of a pair of deep blue eyes fixed upon her in concern.

"You should not have gotten up," Alan declared, and the human sympathy in his voice brought a lump in her throat. She saw his clear-cut features, wavy dark hair, and whimsical mouth through a mist which she strove to wink away. "I'm afraid you have overdone things a bit."

Miriam shook her head. "I could not rest in my bedroom," she said. "There must be something that I can do, Doctor Roberts; unless you distrust me too much." Her voice shook with feeling, and she paused abruptly, unable to go on.

The two men exchanged glances, then Roberts rose. "There, there!" he exclaimed, a trifle awkwardly. "Just take things quietly, Miss Ward, while Alan asks you a few questions. It is his business, you know."

"Just so." Alan Mason nodded reassuringly. "I'm a reporter and also a cousin of Paul's; in fact, his nearest relative. How did Paul seem last night—before you fell asleep?"

"He—" Her pause was infinitesimal. "He appeared much excited, even irrational, but at times his mind was perfectly clear. He took a little nourishment." She stopped and passed one hand before her eyes. Her dreams still haunted her. Could she truthfully say where imagination had dovetailed with reality? Was Betty Carter's visit, her marriage to Paul Abbott but a figment of her overcharged brain? Would her hearers think her a lunatic as well as criminally negligent if she went into details?

Doctor Roberts broke the pause. "I have looked over your chart," he stated, "and find that the last entry was made soon after midnight. You made no record of any marked change in his condition."

Miriam swallowed hard. "The collapse must have come suddenly," she said. "At what time do you think he died?"

Roberts eyed her in silence for a minute. "Come over to the bed," he directed, and not waiting for her, turned on his heel.

The long side curtains of the four-post bedstead were stretched across it, and as Miriam laid her hand on one of them to draw it aside, Alan Mason checked her.

"I found this wad of cotton under the bed," he began. "Had you any occasion last night to use chloroform?"

"No." Miriam looked at him in startled wonder. "No."

"Then," Roberts scanned her closely, "how comes it that you, a trained nurse, are unaware that you were chloroformed?"

Slowly Miriam took in the meaning of his words. "Chloroformed?" she gasped. "*I?*"

It was Alan Mason who answered and not Doctor Roberts. "I detected the odor of chloroform when I carried you to your bedroom," he said. "So then I came in here—found my cousin, Paul, dead—and this cotton under the bed."

Miriam stared at her companions in dumbfounded silence for a moment. "My attack of nausea—" she faltered.

"Was the result of the chloroform," declared Doctor Roberts. His voice deepened. "We also detected its odor about Paul Abbott."

"Good God!" Miriam drew back. "Was Mr. Abbott anesthetized?"

Roberts' gaze never left her face in the lengthened pause.

"In Heaven's name, why don't you answer?" Miriam looked piteously from one man to the other. "Was Mr. Abbott chloroformed?"

"No," replied Roberts. "He was stabbed in the back."

Dragging aside the curtains, Miriam gazed in horror at the bed. The bedclothes had been pulled back and Paul Abbott lay upon his face. Under his left shoulder blade was a dark and sinister bloodstain.

CHAPTER III
COMPLICATIONS

ALAN MASON stopped his restless pacing back and forth and looked at his watch—two o'clock. Surely, the autopsy must be over! He had waited for what appeared an interminable time for the County coroner, his assistant and Doctor Roberts to join him in the living room as they had promised. The afternoon papers would soon be off the press and distributed to the public; it would not be long before the reporters from the other local papers and even the representatives of the great news services located in the National Capital would be at Abbott's Lodge in search of the sensational. And they would find it! Alan's lips were compressed in a hard line. Only six months before he and his cousin, Paul Abbott, had been the closest of "buddies," then had come the estrangement and now death.

Paul had been a social favorite, liked by one and all, and while he had absented himself from Washington during the past year, his tragic death would come as a great shock to his many friends. And Betty Carter—what of her? Alan raised his hands to his temples and brushed his unruly hair upward until it stood on end. The action did not bring any solution of his problems, and with a groan he resumed his restless walk about the living room.

In remodeling the house, Paul Abbott, Senior, had thrown several small rooms into one, also taking down the partitions which inclosed the old-fashioned square staircase, and made the whole into a combination of hallway and living room. He had shown excellent taste in furnishing the old house, using in most instances the mahogany which had been in the family for generations, and when necessary to purchase other pieces of furniture he had hunted in highways and byways for genuine antiques.

But Alan was in no frame of mind to appreciate rare pieces of Hepplewhite, Sheraton, and Chippendale. Tired of the monotony of his surroundings, he strolled into the dining room and walked moodily across it, intending to pour out a glass of water from a carafe on the sideboard. The room was square in shape, with two bow windows and a door leading into a sunparlor which, in summer, the elder Abbott had used as a breakfast room, as the large pantry gave access into it as well as into the regular dining room. From where he stood by the sideboard, Alan could overlook, through one of the bow windows, the garden entrance to the sunparlor. The snow had formed in high drifts, covering completely the rosebushes which, as he recollected, surrounded a plot of grass in the center of which stood an old sundial. It also was blanketed in snow.

As he gazed idly out of the window, Alan saw the door of the sunparlor swing slowly outward. The piled-up snow caused it to jam and he watched with some amusement the efforts of Corbin, the caretaker, to squeeze his portly frame through the partly open door. Once outside Corbin used his snow shovel with vigorous strokes until he had cleared the topmost step. Closing the door to the sunparlor, he leaned his shovel against it, took out his pipe, lighted it, tossed away the match, and drawing on his woolen mitts, he wiped the snow from one of the panes of window glass. Pausing deliberately he glanced about him, and then, cupping his hands, he pressed them against the window and peered inside the sunparlor. Something furtive in the man's action claimed Alan's attention, and he drew back into the protection of the window curtain. The precaution was unnecessary. Corbin straightened up and without a glance at the dining room window, took from his pocket a small metal case. Whatever its contents it drew a smile so evil that Alan stared at the man aghast. He had not been prepossessed in the man's favor on the few occasions when visiting Paul Abbott, Senior, and his son before the war, and had wondered at Paul retaining him in his employ after his father's death.

Returning the case to his pocket, Corbin cleaned the snow from the remaining steps and commenced to shovel a path toward the kitchen. He had almost completed the distance when he paused, stared thoughtfully around him, and then walked back to the sunparlor, clambered cumbersomely up the steps to the door and again peered inside. Fully two minutes passed before he stepped down and walked along the shoveled path.

His curiosity piqued by the man's behavior, Alan waited until Corbin had disappeared from sight, then, turning on his heel, he entered the sunparlor. Evidently Paul had used the room as a lounge, for the wicker furniture, with its attractive cretonne covering, looked homelike and comfortable. Magazines, several books, and a smoking set were on the nearest table, while flower boxes on two sides of the sunparlor added a touch of the tropics, with their hothouse plants. Alan walked past a wicker sofa and several wing chairs grouped at one end and halted abruptly at sight of Miriam Ward lying asleep in one of the long lounging chairs. She had not heard him enter, for she slept on—the deep sleep, as Alan judged from her heavy breathing, of utter exhaustion.

Alan turned and stared about the sunparlor. Except for himself and the trained nurse, the room was empty. What then had absorbed Corbin's attention? Could it have been Miss Ward? He easily detected the particular pane of glass through which the caretaker had peered so intently. Miss Ward was seated directly in its line of vision. What was there about the nurse to make Corbin evince such interest in her?

Alan drew a step closer and stared at the sleeping girl with critical eyes. A little above the medium height of women, slender, well proportioned, her small feet shod in perfectly fitting low white shoes, which showed a very pretty ankle, she lay snuggled down in the cushions. He noted the clear olive of her skin, the deep dimple, almost a cleft, in her chin, the long, heavy lashes, the delicate arch of her finely marked eyebrows, and the soft and abundant hair, which she wore low on her forehead. He judged her to be not over twenty-six and wondered at the pathetic droop of her small mouth. Even in repose there was a suggestion of sadness, of hidden tragedy in her face which, recalling the beauty of her dark eyes, rekindled the interest he had felt in Miriam Ward at their first meeting.

His impulse to awaken her was checked by the thought that she needed the nap—probably the first sound sleep that she had had since coming on the case. It would be cruel to awaken her unnecessarily. Turning about he tiptoed back into the dining room. The sound of his name being softly called caused him to hasten into the living room. Looking up the staircase he saw Doctor Roberts leaning over the banisters and beckoning to him. Taking the stairs two at a time, Alan was by his side in an instant.

"Well," he asked breathlessly. "What news? Have you performed the autopsy?"

"Yes. Come into Paul's bedroom," and as he spoke Roberts led the way across the hall.

Two men were in the bedroom and they both glanced around at the opening of the door. The County Coroner, Doctor James Dixon, Alan knew but slightly; the other, Guy Trenholm, had been his companion on many a hunting trip in the past. Trenholm was of giant stature, with the arms and brawn of the prize ring. There was a certain look in his gray eyes, however, which indicated power of mind as well as physical strength. The son of the town drunkard, Trenholm had spent the first twenty years of his life doing odd chores for the farmers thereabouts and gaining a checkered education, finally acquiring enough money to see him through four years at the University of Maryland. He had been one of the first to enlist upon the entrance of the United States into the World War and at its close had returned to Upper Marlboro with an established record as a "first class fighting man." For nearly a year he had held the office of county sheriff. He greeted Alan with a silent nod and a handclasp, the strength of which made the latter wince.

"Hello, Mason!" exclaimed Coroner Dixon, hustling forward. "I'd no idea you were in these parts again. Your cousin's death is most distressing."

"And a great shock," added Alan soberly. "I was very fond of Paul. We were pals, you know."

"I understood that you two had quarreled," broke in Roberts, then observing Alan's frown, he added hastily: "Forgive me, I did not mean to hurt you by alluding to a painful incident."

"Whatever my feeling in the past, I can harbor no resentment now," retorted Alan, his quick temper ruffled by Roberts' mention of an unhappy memory. "Well, gentlemen, what is the result of the autopsy?"

"Are you asking as a newspaper man or as next of kin?" inquired Coroner Dixon, regarding Alan's flushed countenance attentively.

"As Paul's cousin," quickly. "Whatever you tell me I will consider strictly confidential."

"In that case,"—Dixon selected a chair—"we held the autopsy in a spare bedroom at the back of the house," observing Alan's eyes stray toward the four-post bedstead, the curtains of which still remained drawn. "The undertaker and his assistants are there now." He sat back and regarded Alan. "We can consult together here without being disturbed. As you know, Mr. Abbott had been ill for several days with an attack of bronchitis and threatened pneumonia; this, coupled with heart complications, made his condition very serious."

"But did either cause his death?" asked Alan.

"No," responded the coroner. "We probed the wound in his back and found that the weapon had penetrated the left lung. In his weakened condition, death must have been instantaneous."

Alan drew a long breath. "So the wound really was fatal!" he exclaimed. "The lack of much blood led me to believe that possibly the weapon had not struck a vital point."

"The hemorrhage was internal." Coroner Dixon's expression grew more serious. "There is no doubt, Mason, but that your cousin was murdered."

Alan passed his hand across his eyes. "My God!" he groaned. "Who harbored such animosity against Paul and how was the murder committed?"

"That is what we have to find out," cut in Sheriff Trenholm. "Where is the nurse who was with Mr. Abbott last night, Doctor Roberts?"

"In her room, I presume—"

"No, she is asleep downstairs," interrupted Alan hastily. "Shall I call her?" A nod from Trenholm was his only answer, and Alan hurried from the room, but at the head of the staircase he caught a glimpse of a white skirt disappearing around the further corner of the hall and he changed his direction. He caught up with Miriam Ward just as she was turning the knob of a closed door, a number of towels in her left hand.

"You are wanted by the coroner," he explained, as she stopped at sight of him.

Miriam grew a shade paler. "Very well," she replied, "But first—" she handed the towels to the undertaker and closed the door again. "Where is the coroner, Mr. Mason?"

"In my cousin's old bedroom." Alan suited his long stride to her shorter one. "I hope you feel a bit rested," glancing down at her with some concern, but it was doubtful if she heard his remark, her attention being centered on a figure coming up the staircase. Alan stopped short as he recognized the newcomer and his face grew stern.

"Betty!" he exclaimed.

She stared at him for a long moment, then without a word of any kind she walked by them and through the bedroom door near which Doctor Roberts was standing, waiting to greet her. Without halting Betty made at once for the four-post bedstead.

"Wait, Betty!" Alan had gained her side and laid a compelling hand on her arm. "Paul is not there."

Betty regarded him in utter silence, then faced about and looked at the small group in the bedroom.

"Paul is dead—dead!" she spoke with great difficulty, one hand plucking always at the collar of her fur coat. "You shall not keep me from him. You—" for a second her blazing eyes scanned Sheriff Trenholm—"you dare not."

"Hush, Betty!" Roberts took the overwrought girl's hand in his. "You shall see Paul later, dear, that I promise you. Sit down and calm yourself."

"I have your word?" Betty's great eyes never left Roberts. "I shall see Paul?"

"Yes. There, sit down," as Miriam Ward pulled forward a chair.

"Perhaps the young lady had better withdraw to another room," suggested Coroner Dixon. "We are about to start an investigation—"

"An investigation?" Betty's high-pitched voice, carrying a warning note of approaching hysteria to Miriam Ward's watchful ears, reached to the hall beyond and a figure crouching near the bedroom door, which had been inadvertently left open a few inches, leaned forward, the better to catch what was transpiring in the room. "What do you mean, sir?"

Coroner Dixon contemplated her for a second in silence. Betty's unusual beauty generally commanded attention, but something in her expression focused the Coroner's regard rather than her good looks, marred as they were by deep circles under her eyes and haggard lines about her mouth. He answered her question with another.

"Your name, madam?" he asked. "And your relation to the dead man?"

"This is Miss Betty Carter," broke in Doctor Roberts. "Mr. Abbott's fiancée."

"Is it so?" Coroner Dixon's interest quickened. "Then Mr. Abbott—"

"Was very dear to me." Betty's tone had grown husky. "I must know all about his death." Her gaze swept Guy Trenholm, standing somewhat in the background. "It is my right."

Coroner Dixon turned and glanced in doubt at Trenholm. At the latter's reassuring nod he faced about.

"Very well, Miss Carter," he began. "Since you insist I will tell you what we have learned." He cleared his voice before continuing. "Judging by the condition of the body, Mr. Abbott died between one-thirty this morning and three o'clock. He was stabbed."

"Stabbed!" With a convulsive movement Betty gained her feet, her face deadly white. "*Stabbed!*"

Doctor Roberts laid a soothing hand on hers. "Be quiet, Betty," he cautioned. "Or you will have to go and lie down."

She shook off his hand. "Go on," she directed, and the urgency of her tone caused Dixon to speak more rapidly.

"Mr. Abbott was stabbed in the back," he stated. "We know no more than that, at present."

Without taking her gaze from the coroner, Betty resumed her seat. Then she turned to Roberts. "I heard yesterday that Paul was very ill, and that you were attending him professionally. Were you with him last night?"

"Yes; until Miss Ward came and then I put her in charge of the case," replied Roberts. "She can tell you what happened after my departure."

Miriam Ward faced their concentrated regard with outward composure. Caught by chance in the web of circumstance, she was keenly alive to her unhappy share in the tragic occurrences of the night before. Having a high regard for her profession and throwing her heart and soul into her work she felt, however little she had been to blame, that the stigma of neglect of a patient would be laid at her door.

"Before leaving, Doctor Roberts gave me full instructions," she began. "And I carried them out. My chart shows that—"

"But your last entry was made shortly after midnight," pointed out Sheriff Trenholm, picking up the chart from the table at his elbow. "Why was that, Miss Ward?"

"I was interrupted by the arrival of Miss Carter," she replied, and the unexpected answer brought a startled exclamation from three of her companions; then their gaze left the nurse and centered on Betty. The latter raised her eyes and regarded the trained nurse. If chiseled from marble, her white face could not have been more devoid of human expression.

"God bless my soul!" ejaculated Doctor Roberts. "What were you doing here, Betty?"

The girl paid not the slightest attention to him; instead she addressed Miriam, and the others were startled at her tone.

"Go on with your story," she said. "Speak quickly," with a glance at her wrist watch. "Time is passing."

"Miss Carter was accompanied by a clergyman." Miriam spoke more slowly, weighing her words. "I—I"—she hesitated for a brief moment—"I cannot recall his name—"

"Continue," directed Dixon, as she paused. "Did Miss Carter and her companion see Mr. Abbott?"

"I think they did;" she hesitated. "I feel sure they did—"

"Why are you in doubt about it?" demanded Trenholm quickly. "Weren't you in the room with them?"

Miriam shook her head. "Not all the time," she admitted. "The clergyman sent me downstairs to get a lamp as the one in this room had burned out. When I came back—"

"Yes—what then?" Sheriff Trenholm could not restrain his impatience at her slow speech.

"The clergyman had just completed the marriage service."

Her words created a sensation. Doctor Roberts' eyes fairly started from his head, and Alan Mason's excited ejaculation drowned Dixon's more softly spoken exclamation. Only Guy Trenholm gave no voice to his feelings. With eyes fixed steadfastly upon Betty, he remained as emotionless apparently as she.

"What transpired next?" inquired Dixon.

"They left," tersely. Miriam's heart was beating quickly, and her cold fingers were playing a devil's tattoo on the arm of her chair. Before she could say more, Betty leaned forward and held up her hand.

"Just a moment!" She spoke slowly, distinctly. "What were you, a trained nurse, doing when your patient was stabbed to death?"

Miriam whitened, but faced her questioner with quiet courage.

"I was lying near the bed unconscious," she admitted, "having been chloroformed."

Betty rose to her feet. "I have heard that a person under the influence of chloroform or ether is subject to hallucinations," she said. "I prefer to believe that than to think you are demented."

"Demented!" Miriam sprang up, her eyes flashing with indignation.

Betty addressed Sheriff Trenholm directly, ignoring the others. "The nurse is either demented or drawing upon her imagination," she declared. "I was not here last night." She faced Miriam and her glance was impersonal, unfaltering. "Nor have I ever seen you before."

CHAPTER IV
THE BLACK CREST

MARTHA CORBIN laid down the brass fire tongs and turned to look at the wood-basket by the hearth. The logs were both long and heavy. Before attempting to lift one her attention was caught by the sound of a familiar lagging footstep going in the direction of the back hall.

"You, Charlie," she called, shrilly. "Come 'ere and fix this fire."

A snarl was his only response, and a second later a door banged shut behind her amiable spouse. Martha's thin lips compressed into a hard line. Stooping over she tugged and pulled at the topmost log and finally lifted it up. She let it fall in the center of the burning wood and then rested one hand against the stone chimney to get her breath. It was some seconds before she felt able to take up the hearth brush and sweep the ashes back under the andirons. That successfully accomplished she dropped on one knee and held her chilled hands up to the blaze. She was grateful for the heat.

As she crouched there the firelight, which alone illuminated the living room at Abbott's Lodge, cast fantastic shadows on her face, exaggerating her fixed expression to one of almost fierce determination. Still in her early forties, Martha Corbin had once been extremely pretty, but ill health had destroyed her good looks and whitened her hair, which, worn straight back, intensified the gray pallor of her appearance.

Her prolonged stare at the fire wavered finally, caught by a piece of white paper protruding from a crack in the tiled hearth. One end was singed, but it had fallen on the outer edge of the bed of hot ashes and escaped entire destruction. Reaching down she picked up the piece and turned it over. It was evidently the upper right-hand corner of an envelope, for the flap still bore traces of glue as well as a perfectly formed black seal—the wax unbroken except at the edges. Martha had no chance to read the printed lines on the reverse of the paper.

"What have ye there?" demanded Corbin over her shoulder and seized her roughly.

With surprising swiftness she broke from his grasp and got to her feet.

"A bit of torn paper," she replied; "from the scrap basket, there," touching it with her foot. "I was emptying it in the fire."

"And didn't the sheriff say you wasn't to touch nothing?" She met his alarmed look with a timid shrug of her shoulders. "Have ye no sense at all?"

Martha favored him with a blank stare as she stood twisting her hands in her apron.

"I had to build up the fire," she mumbled. "'Twas only an old newspaper and such like rubbish."

"Ye hadn't oughter touched it," he growled. "Suppose Sheriff Trenholm or one of his men ask for the basket?"

"Well, here 'tis." With a swift glance about them, she darted over to a chair and taking up a newspaper lying upon it, crumpled it up and thrust it into the scrap basket. Hurrying to the mahogany desk she jerked open one of the drawers and drew out a bundle of letters and tossed it into the basket also.

"Have a care, Martha!" exclaimed Corbin, who had followed her rapid movements in startled silence. "There's to be a search and everything in Abbott's Lodge examined by the sheriff."

"He'll find the newspaper and the letters in the scrap basket as easy as if they were on the chair or in the drawer," she remarked, smiling shrewdly. "'Twon't matter *where* they find 'em." She smoothed down the torn hem of her large apron and drew closer to her husband. "What do ye 'spose he done with it?"

"Sh!" He clapped his scarred hand across her lips. "Hold your tongue, woman. They'll hear, mebbe."

"Nobody to hear," she replied tersely, drawing away from him. "Mr. Alan is seeing Coroner Dixon off and Miss Betty Carter is still upstairs in the room with *him*!" She shivered. "Ain't it *awful* the way she's taking on?"

Corbin nodded, half absently, his eyes intent on scanning the living room and its staircase at its other end.

"Surprising, after we know what happened," he admitted, speaking in little more than a whisper. "But, recollect, Martha, 'tain't up to us to *talk*. If ye do"—His look caused her to catch her breath. "Well, ye know what's coming to ye. Ye understand"—and he seized her arm and turned it until she winced with pain.

"Leave me be!" She winced again as Corbin, with a final twist, released her arm. "You've no call to handle me so."

Corbin's only answer was a vicious scowl and Martha shrank back, one hand to her trembling lips.

"I don't need to speak twice," he commented. "*You* know me."

She nodded dumbly as she retreated behind a chair.

"Did ye hear when the nurse was leaving?" she asked.

The question went unanswered as Corbin, his attention attracted by voices on the floor above, slipped noiselessly down the passageway through which he had entered some minutes earlier unseen by his wife. Left to her own devices, Martha picked up a box of matches and lighted one of the lamps. She had succeeded in adjusting the wick when she looked up and caught sight of Betty Carter regarding her from the lower landing of the staircase.

"Light the others," Betty directed. "All of them—every one"—indicating with a wave of her hand the standing lamp at the foot of the stairs and several reading lamps placed on small tables near comfortable lounging chairs where Paul Abbott and his guests had been wont to pass the long winter evenings. Betty waited on the stair landing until her peremptory order had been carried out, then slowly approached the fireplace. She turned back on reaching there and addressed Martha.

"Take my coat," she said, extending it. "And my hat"—She removed it as she spoke. "And prepare a bedroom for me."

"A what, Miss?"

"A bedroom. I propose staying here to-night."

Martha gazed at her as if she had not heard aright. "Here, Miss?" she faltered. "Here?"

"Certainly." Betty regarded the frightened woman more attentively. "Do as I tell you." Her sharp tone aroused Martha from her startled contemplation of her. "You can take my hat and coat upstairs as you go and hang them in the bedroom closet. Come, what's the matter with you?"

"Nothing, Miss, nothing." Martha reached out a reluctant hand and took the proffered coat and hat, then without further word she hastened up the staircase. So great was her speed that she stumbled breathlessly into a bedroom halfway down the corridor of the second floor, the door of which stood partly open.

Miriam Ward turned at her unceremonious entrance and regarded her in astonishment.

"What is it?" she asked, alarmed at the woman's pallor. "Are you ill?"

Martha shook her head as she advanced to the closet and, opening the door, disappeared inside, to reappear the next instant, empty-handed.

"No, ma'am, I ain't ill," she volunteered, resting one hand on the chair-back. "But I think she are."

"She? Who?"

"Miss Betty Carter." Martha breathed more easily. "She says she is going to stay here all night."

Miriam stared at the woman. "Well, what of it?" she asked. "Why shouldn't she stay if she wishes to?"

"All by her lonesome and Mr. Paul lying here dead!" Martha's voice of disapproval registered a higher key than her usual monotone. "Who is going to watch after her? That is," catching herself up, "look after her?"

"You, I suppose," replied Miriam. "Are you not accustomed to doing the housework?"

"Sure." Martha's voice grew more natural. "And Mr. Paul always said I was a prime cook. Say, Miss Ward, ye ain't going, are ye?"

"Very shortly, yes." Miriam Ward returned to the table on which stood her leather bag which she had been packing when interrupted by Martha, and laid in it her neatly folded white uniform. The metal case containing hypodermic syringe, thermometer, and small phials of stimulants was next tucked carefully inside, and then Miriam closed and locked the bag. "Have you seen Doctor Roberts recently?"

Martha shook her head. "He is still about the place with Mr. Alan," she responded. She cocked an inquisitive eye at Miriam and took in appraisingly her trim, well-cut wool house gown. She had a dim, preconceived notion that all nurses were dowdy, and to find Miriam a becomingly dressed, extremely pretty, well-bred young woman was a distinct novelty. "Are ye going into Washington with Doctor Roberts?"

"Yes. He asked me to wait for him." Miriam was conscious of a feeling of repulsion under the steady stare of Martha's oddly matched eyes—the iris of one was a pale blue, while the other was a deep brown. "I have not slept in the bed, Martha; so it is not necessary for you to remake it"—as the housekeeper laid her hand on the white counterpane. "But perhaps it would be just as well to have your husband bring up more wood. The room is a trifle chilly."

"There's some in the wood box in the hall; I'll get it"—and before Miriam could utter a remonstrance, Martha had hurried away. She was back again in an instant, her arms full of small blocks of cord wood. Not waiting for Miriam's quickly proffered assistance, she let them fall clumsily on the hearth, and then gazed aghast at a long rent in her apron in which still hung a sliver of wood. Her name, called with loud insistence in her husband's unmistakable accents, caused her to start violently. Pausing only long enough to untie her apron and toss it aside, she hurried from the room, jostling Miriam in her haste to be gone.

Miriam stood in thought for a few seconds, then moved over to the pier glass and put on her hat. She regretted having accepted Doctor Roberts' invitation to drive to the city with him. Had she followed her own inclination, she would have ordered a taxicab immediately after her scene with Betty Carter and departed. But, confused by Betty's, to her, incomprehensible behavior, she had listened to Coroner Dixon's urgent request that she remain a few hours longer at Abbott's lodge, until, as he expressed it, Betty had had time to pull herself together. Coroner Dixon hinted that hysteria explained her conduct. Miriam's expression grew more thoughtful. The shock of finding her lover dead might account for much, but was that *alone* responsible for Betty's denial of her midnight visit to Abbott's Lodge?

Sheriff Trenholm had summed up the situation in one brief sentence—"It's one girl's word against the other."

And she, "the other girl," was unknown and without money, while Betty had hosts of friends and an assured position in the world!

If she could only recall the name of the clergyman who had accompanied Betty! He would substantiate her statement. But try as she did to clearly remember each event of the night, his name eluded her. Undoubtedly the chloroform, with which she had been anesthetized, had much to do with her loss of memory. With proper rest, its effects would undoubtedly wear off; until then—

Miriam fingered the string of blue beads, which she was wearing, nervously. Neither Coroner Dixon nor Sheriff Trenholm had given her an inkling as to whether they really placed faith in her statement. They had listened with deep interest and without comment. In the face of their silence, she had hesitated to tell them of finding a strange man and not her patient in Abbott's bed just before she lost consciousness. With no proof to offer them, she feared the hard-headed Sheriff would consider her demented indeed.

Turning from the mirror, Miriam walked across the bedroom toward the chair on which she had laid her coat and inadvertently trod on Martha's discarded apron. As she lifted it up, intending to put it on the chair, a piece of paper rolled out of a rip in the hem of the apron and fell at her feet. Instinctively Miriam stooped over and picked up the paper, but instead of laying it down on top of the apron, she continued to hold it in front of her, her eyes caught by a black seal. The wax impression of the crest was distinct and unmistakable. With a sharp intake of her breath, Miriam turned over the half burned envelope. The Canadian postage was intact, but the name of the person to whom the envelope had been addressed was entirely burned away.

Miriam continued to regard the piece of envelope with fixed intentness. Slowly she deciphered the blurred postmark—it bore a recent date, of that she was positive—but then, how came the black crest upon any letter? Who dared to use it? Miriam was conscious of a feeling of icy coldness not due to the temperature of the room.

An authoritative tap on her door brought the red blood to her white cheeks with a rush and as Alan Mason looked inside the room at her low-voiced, "Come in," he was struck by her air of distinction and the direct gaze of her hazel eyes, which were her chief beauty.

"Doctor Roberts is about to leave," he said. "Let me carry your bag," as she made a motion toward it, "and your coat." Not listening to her murmured protest, he gathered up her things and waited for her to precede him through the doorway.

Miriam's hesitation was imperceptible. Opening her handbag she dropped the half burned envelope inside it, then composedly walked down the corridor. At the head of the staircase she paused and addressed her companion.

"Have they made any plans for the funeral?" she asked.

"It is postponed until after the preliminary hearing of the inquest," Alan replied, keeping his voice lowered.

"And has that been called?"

He nodded. "For to-morrow morning, I understand. There is some technicality which is causing unexpected delay." They were almost at the bottom of the stairs when he caught sight of Betty Carter standing in front of the fireplace talking to Doctor Roberts. Alan ceased speaking with such abruptness that he drew an inquiring glance from Miriam, of which he was totally unaware. Doctor Roberts gave her no time for thought, however. Coming hastily forward, he reached her side in time to help her on with her coat.

"I am sorry to have kept you waiting," he said. "But there were certain matters.... Bless my soul, Alan, more reporters!" as the gong over the front door sounded with startling suddenness. "Betty, my dear," turning to address the silent girl by the fireplace, "you had better disappear if you don't wish to be interviewed."

"I'll see them; don't worry," exclaimed Alan, as he swung open the front door. But instead of the anticipated reporters, he was confronted by a small familiar figure bundled up in expensive furs. "Mrs. Nash!"

"Just so!" Mrs. Nash lowered the high collar of her coat as she came further into the living room, and collapsed in the nearest chair. "Let me get my breath. Dear me, I'm half frozen!" and she chafed one cold hand over the other. "Come here, Betty, and help me off with these things."

"Why, Aunt Dora!" Betty hastened to her side. "How imprudent of you to come all the way out here! You will surely be ill."

"I haven't a doubt of it," declared Mrs. Nash, through chattering teeth. "I got out of a sick bed to come here, and Pierre, the wretch, ran out of gasoline a mile away and I had to walk through the snow or sit in the car and freeze to death. Good gracious, Alan! don't stand there looking at me; get me something warm to drink. I am having a chill."

"A hot water bag, also," added Doctor Roberts, hastening to her assistance as Mrs. Nash struggled out of her coat.

"I can find whisky more easily than the latter," answered Alan, and sped for the dining room. Miriam Ward was close behind him and helped him pour out a generous allowance from the carefully concealed decanter.

"I saw a hot water bag hanging in your cousin's bathroom," she said. "I will get it and have it filled if you will give this stimulant to Mrs. Nash." She paused by the door. "Is Mrs. Nash's husband a clergyman?"

"Yes. Why?" glancing keenly at her flushed cheeks.

"Nothing—that is," avoiding his gaze. "Don't keep Mrs. Nash waiting," as she hurried away with a fast beating heart. She had recalled the name of Betty's companion on her midnight visit to Paul Abbott—Doctor Nash.

Mrs. Nash accepted the proffered whisky with relief. "I need a bracer," she admitted. "Indeed, Betty, the shocking news of poor Paul's untimely death bowled me over; and then to be told that you had raced out here in a hired taxi, without either your uncle or me,—it—it—took my breath away." A shiver which she could not check shook her from head to foot and Doctor Roberts helped her to a couch, while Betty brought a heavy laprobe and threw it over her aunt. As she turned away Mrs. Nash caught Doctor Roberts' coat sleeve and motioned to him to bend down.

"Is it really true," she questioned him in a whisper, "that Paul has been murdered?"

"Yes. Hush, no details now," as Miriam approached the couch. He addressed her in his customary tone of voice. "Ah, a hot water bag; just the thing. You are fortunate, Mrs. Nash, in having a trained nurse right here at your elbow."

"Thank you!" Mrs. Nash's piercing black eyes took in Miriam's appearance in a pronounced stare. She permitted Miriam to make herself more comfortable, before addressing her again. "Have you been nursing Mr. Abbott?"

"Yes." Miriam stepped back from the couch and turned to Doctor Roberts. "I think I had better telephone for a taxi."

"And my aunt can return to Washington with you," broke in Betty Carter as she joined the small group. "It will be an excellent arrangement."

"I make my own plans, thank you," retorted Mrs. Nash, whose high color betokened a touch of temper. "Do you suppose that with this attack of flu I can venture out of doors again?"

"You don't mean to say you propose to spend the night here?" asked Alan, returning in time to hear her last remark.

"Certainly. My husband and I have been frequent visitors, and I know there are plenty of bedrooms."

"But, my dear Aunt, suppose you get sick?" Betty gazed at her in utter disapproval.

"I am sick already," declared Mrs. Nash. "Chills and fever—where's your thermometer, Doctor?"

Roberts looked grave as he prepared the small instrument for her.

"Your niece is right," he said. "This country place is isolated from Washington in winter, and with illness—" he paused to put the thermometer in Mrs. Nash's mouth; then he addressed Betty. "I think you also had better change your plan, and return to Washington."

"I am the best judge of what I should do," she huffed and turned away. Roberts eyed her in speculative silence as he took out his fountain pen and wrote a prescription.

Alan, who had been watching Betty also, turned to Miriam. "Where can the coroner reach you?" he asked. "You have not given me your address? Or let me have your bill?" he added, lowering his voice to a confidential pitch.

Miriam colored warmly; the commercial side of her profession always embarrassed her. "I was engaged for an eighteen-hour duty," she stammered. "I suppose the charge is seven dollars."

Alan drew out his wallet and pressed some bills into her hand. "And your address?" he asked eagerly.

"You can always reach me through Central Registry," and with a nod of gratitude she passed him to go to the telephone.

From her couch, Mrs. Nash watched her opportunity. With a gesture of surprising quickness she removed the thermometer from her mouth and tucked it unseen against the hot water bottle. When Doctor Roberts closed his notebook and turned back to her, the thermometer was once again held firmly between her lips. He took it out, looked at it twice, and then at Mrs. Nash's scarlet countenance.

"Miss Ward," he called, and his voice was grave. "Don't order a taxi—I think that you had better remain and prepare a bedroom for Mrs. Nash," and then, in an undertone, as Miriam gained his side, "it will never do to take Mrs. Nash out in this weather—her temperature reads 103°."

CHAPTER V
SHERIFF TRENHOLM ASKS QUESTIONS

A DISTINCT and unmistakable snore from the bed caused Miriam to approach her patient. Mrs. Nash, her head unevenly balanced between two pillows, was at last asleep. To place her in a more comfortable position would undoubtedly awaken her, and Miriam backed away on tiptoe from the bedside. She had spent three weary hours at Mrs. Nash's beck and call; she had run every conceivable errand the sick woman's fancy had dictated, had prepared her for bed, and finally induced her, on threat of departure, to swallow the medicine prescribed by Doctor Roberts.

Martha's scanty wardrobe could not provide clothing for Mrs. Nash, and the housekeeper had been dispatched to Upper Marlboro, the county seat, in the Nash limousine which had finally put in an appearance, to purchase such necessities as the country stores could supply. Betty Carter had taken little part in the discussion, contenting herself with the request that Martha buy a wrapper, bedroom slippers, and a night dress and bring them at once to her room, whereupon she had gone upstairs and locked her door. Martha had carried her dinner to her upon her return from the shopping expedition.

Miriam had been too intent upon her professional duties to pay much attention to the other members of the small party, but she had gathered from Martha's remarks that Alan Mason and Doctor Roberts had left for Upper Marlboro in the latter's car shortly after dinner. Martha, with a sidelong glance which Miriam was beginning to associate with the housekeeper's personality, had overheard Alan tell her husband that he would return in time to "sit up with Mr. Paul."

"Ain't it awful, Ma'am—Miss, to think of that poor gentleman lying in t'other room dead," she went on, with a shiver. "And him so sot on getting well. Poor Mr. Paul!" And she wiped away a few tears with the hem of her clean apron. "He won't rest easy in his grave."

The housekeeper's words recurred to Miriam as her gaze, which had been wandering about the room, rested on a small, black-bordered sketch of what appeared to be a group of neglected graves. The picture was well executed, but Miriam wondered at its selection for a decoration in a bedroom. From the drawing Miriam's eyes wandered to several paintings on the wall, and, from the likeness of one of the portraits to Paul Abbott, she judged it to be that of his father. Evidently the room given to Mrs. Nash had once been occupied by the elder Abbott, whether as bedroom or sitting room was hard to say, for the remainder of the pictures on the wall were hunting scenes and, except for the bedstead, the rest of the furniture was such as is found in a man's "den."

Miriam selected the most comfortable of the easy-chairs and, taking care to make no noise, pushed it around so that from its depths she could have an unobstructed view of her patient. Her fatigued muscles relaxed as she sank back in the chair, but her brain—ah, it was on fire! For a moment she looked with envy at the slumbering woman. If she could only sleep as soundly with no visions of the past to disturb her! The present was bad enough in all conscience—who could have murdered Paul Abbott and what possible motive could have inspired the crime?

The cautious turning of the door knob and the slow opening of the door caused her to bend forward in her chair. Sheriff Trenholm leaned inside the door and, catching sight of Miriam, raised a beckoning finger, and then placed it against his lips, enjoining silence.

Miriam's rubber-soled shoes made no noise on the hardwood floor and she gained the hall door without disturbing her patient.

"What is it?" she asked, stepping partly into the hall, down which the sheriff had retreated a few paces.

"I'd like to have a talk with you," he replied. "Just quietly, by ourselves."

"But my patient!" she exclaimed.

"She is asleep, isn't she?"

"Yes, but—" She came further into the hall so as to speak more emphatically and yet not awaken Mrs. Nash. "I am on night duty. I cannot leave my patient alone."

"You don't have to; Mrs. Corbin will stay with her, and call you if there is the slightest need for your presence." Sheriff Trenholm moved to one side and Miriam caught a glimpse beyond him of Martha loitering by the door to Paul Abbott's old bedroom. "Come, Miss Ward, you will only be across the corridor from Mrs. Nash; and it is essential that I see you to-night." His voice deepened and his hand, as if by accident, pulled back his coat so that the badge of authority on his vest was visible. "I'll relieve you of any responsibility should Mrs. Nash question your absence," he added. "Go in, Mrs. Corbin," as the housekeeper, who had drawn nearer, paused undecidedly.

Miriam stepped back into the bedroom. Mrs. Nash was still asleep—there was really nothing left for her to do but obey the sheriff. She turned to Martha, standing timidly half in and half out of the room.

"Sit over in that chair," she directed softly, indicating the one she had occupied a moment before. "If Mrs. Nash grows restless in her sleep or wakens, come at once for me."

"Yes, Ma'am—Miss." Martha found it difficult to decide on her mode of address so far as the nurse was concerned, and compromised the matter by jumbling the titles together. "Don't ye be afeared; I'll call ye."

Sheriff Trenholm was standing in the center of Abbott's old bedroom staring at the windows, the curtains of which were drawn. He turned around at Miriam's entrance and, stepping behind her, closed the hall door.

"I don't wish our talk to be interrupted," he said by way of explanation. "Now, Miss Ward, exactly what occurred here last night?"

Miriam studied the man in front of her in silence. There was something big and fine about Guy Trenholm—an air of candor, of strength—that impressed her, but an inborn caution, a streak inherited from some dour Scottish ancestor, kept back the words on her tongue. Suppose the sheriff was setting a trap for her?

"Will I be called as a witness at the inquest?" she asked.

"Sure."

"Then why question me now?"

His smile was friendly as he pulled forward a chair and stood resting one hand on it. "The inquest may be delayed a few days," he explained. "There is a conflict of authority as to jurisdiction"—he paused, then added more briskly: "Is the furniture in this room placed as it was last night?"

Miriam stared about her before answering. "It is just the same," she said.

"And the windows?"

"Two were open." She crossed the room and laid her hand on a tall mahogany screen. "I placed this here so that the air would not blow directly on Mr. Abbott and arranged the curtains at that window so as to protect him also."

Trenholm walked by her and, raising the window nearest the four-post bedstead, looked outside. "It gives on the roof of the verandah," he said, drawing in his head. "An easy climb from the ground for an agile man. It is a reasonable hypothesis that the murderer gained entrance that way."

"Wouldn't he have left tracks in the snow?" she broke in quickly.

"He probably did, but there was a second fall of snow about five this morning which obliterated all marks." The sheriff closed the window. "This screen made an admirable hiding place, I have no doubt. He probably sprang from behind it and chloroformed you."

Miriam shivered. "When I came to myself this morning I was lying just about here"—she pointed with her foot to a spot midway between the bed and the screen.

"And you detected no sound—no odd noises when the murderer entered the room?" questioned Trenholm and his gaze never left her face.

"I heard nothing to make me suspect that any one was in the room except Mr. Abbott and me," she stated. "You recollect that I was absent several times; once when I went downstairs to admit Miss Betty Carter and her companion," she hesitated. "And when I went to the head of the staircase at their departure." Again she hesitated. "I also left the room on an errand while they were here."

Trenholm eyed her oddly. "What was the errand and who sent you on it?"

"The lamp went out and the clergyman asked me to get one from downstairs," she explained, tersely.

He considered her statements for several moments, then nodded his head thoughtfully. "The man probably selected one of the times when Paul was left alone—preferably the last occasion, for then there was less danger of detection. You were chloroformed immediately upon your return?"

"Y-yes. I lost consciousness—I—" Her hesitation caught his attention. "It is all very confused; I cannot think clearly."

"Brace up!" His tone, though kindly, was firm, and Miriam checked her inclination to cry—she was utterly weary and her head ached with memories which would not down. "Now," he added as she bit her lip and winked back the tears. "Are you positive you heard no one talking to Mr. Abbott?"

"Except Miss Carter."

"Well, aside from her," with patient persistence.

Miriam shook her head. "I can swear that I heard no one converse with Mr. Abbott except Doctor Roberts and Miss Carter."

"There was no murmur of voices as you lost consciousness?"

"I heard none."

"Strange!" mused Trenholm. "Why did not Paul Abbott cry out when you were chloroformed? He was conscious last night—?"

"Oh, yes, although occasionally irrational." She glanced up at the sheriff and then toward the bed. "Possibly he was killed before I returned."

"That may be." Trenholm tugged at his mustache. "Was Mr. Abbott in a condition to get up?"

"He might have, with assistance," cautiously.

He regarded her in silence, then nodded his head. "That is what Doctor Roberts told me." Again he stroked his mustache. "Have you examined the bed since the body was removed?"

"No."

"Then look here." He walked with her to the four-post bedstead and drew aside the curtains. The blankets and top sheet were neatly pulled back, leaving exposed the under sheet, while the pillows lay as Miriam had last seen them. "Do you notice that there are no marks of blood, except this small stain," motioning toward a spot near the head of the bed.

Miriam bent over the bedclothes and then looked up at the sheriff.

"I found Mr. Abbott lying partly on his left side—"

"He wasn't stabbed in that position," declared Trenholm vehemently. "It would have been a physical impossibility—"

"Unless the murderer stood facing him as he lay in bed and, reaching over Mr. Abbott's shoulder, stabbed him in the back," suggested Miriam.

Trenholm looked doubtful. "That is possible but not probable," he retorted. "And it is not borne out by facts. If he was killed in bed, the sheets would have been stained with blood."

His remark was caught by Alan Mason as the latter stepped inside the bedroom. At the sound of his entrance, Trenholm wheeled around and his frown at the interruption gave place to a pleased smile. Alan bowed to Miriam before addressing the sheriff.

"Coroner Dixon told me that the wound bled internally," he pointed out. "Wouldn't that explain the comparatively stainless condition of the sheets?"

"Not to my way of thinking," declared the sheriff. He frowned again. "No, I don't believe Paul was killed in that bed."

"Do you mean that the murderer lifted Paul out of bed, killed him, and then put him back in bed?" Alan smiled in derision as he put the question. "Come, that's absurd."

"Wait!" Miriam drew a step nearer Alan. His presence gave her courage. There was something indefinable about Alan Mason which, for want of a better word, she recognized as caste. His consideration in having a dinner tray sent to Mrs. Nash's door had kept her from a supperless vigil in the sick room and it was but one of many small acts of courtesy. "There is something I must tell you."

"Yes? Go on, Miss Ward." Sheriff Trenholm brought her a chair. "Sit down, you must be worn out."

Mechanically she seated herself. "I wanted to tell you this afternoon," she continued, struggling to steady her voice. She felt strangely nervous. Surely the curtains of the four-post bedstead were moving? She looked hard at them, then averted her gaze. Pshaw, nerves must not get the best of her. "But Miss Carter insisted that I was demented."

Alan changed his weight from one foot to the other as he leaned against the table. "Miss Carter appeared hardly accountable for her behavior," he began. "I think that we can safely say that, eh, Guy?"

Sheriff Trenholm did not at once reply. With head bent he studied the pattern of the rug upon which they were standing, and when he looked up his expression was inscrutable.

"Miss Carter will be questioned further," he said noncommittally. "Go ahead, Miss Ward."

Miriam Ward moistened her dry lips. Would they believe her, or would she simply involve herself more deeply in the mystery by making statements which she could not prove?

"When I came back after Miss Carter's departure with her companion," she spoke slowly, almost haltingly, and to one of the men watching her, she appeared more like an animated waxen figure than a human being, "I put down the lamp and walked over to this bed. The curtains were adjusted about as they are now." Miriam paused and pointed toward them. "I drew them aside and looked down—a strange man lay in the bed."

With one accord the two men advanced to her side. "Where was Paul?" demanded Alan and the sheriff almost in the same breath.

"I do not know," replied Miriam. "The shock of not seeing my patient was so great I felt myself reeling backwards—and knew no more."

Guy Trenholm and Alan exchanged glances. "And the murderer's confederate seized that moment to chloroform you!" ejaculated Alan.

"Confederate? You are traveling fast, Alan, my boy," exclaimed Trenholm. "Why couldn't the man in the bed have sprung up as Miss Ward toppled over and chloroformed her as she lay on the floor in a fainting condition?"

"That is possible," agreed Alan. "What did the man look like, Miss Ward?"

Miriam's gaze shifted dumbly from one to the other of her companions. She had dreaded the question. "His eyes were closed and except that he wore a beard and his hair was dark, I cannot tell you what he looked like," she stammered. "The room was dimly lighted. I saw the man but for an instant, and then lost consciousness."

Sheriff Trenholm regarded her in steadfast silence. It was Alan who broke the prolonged pause.

"Would you know the man if you saw him again?" he asked and Miriam was grateful that no note of doubt had crept into his voice.

"I am sure I would," she answered swiftly.

"Then, don't worry." Alan's smile was very engaging. His eyes swept a searching glance about the big bedroom. "How was the man dressed?"

Miriam shook her head. "I have no idea. The bedclothes were pulled up about his shoulders to his chin." She hesitated. "I only caught a glimpse of his profile."

CHAPTER VI
THE THIRD HAND

THE minutes dragged interminably to Martha Corbin and she wished most devoutly that she had gone to her room before Guy Trenholm had found her in the kitchen. The sheriff was not a man to disobey, and at his peremptory direction she had at once accompanied him upstairs to find Miriam Ward. But she had not bargained on having to take the nurse's place in Mrs. Nash's bedroom. Illness in any form terrified her, and only the knowledge that Miriam was across the hall kept her in her chair. At first she had not been uncomfortable, but as Miriam's absence grew prolonged, the housekeeper found it impossible to keep still. Her twitching fingers fumbled with the arms of the tufted chair until she had loosened four or five upholstery buttons and pulled off several inches of braid. Bouncing to her feet she looked at Mrs. Nash, then, convinced that she was still asleep, she tiptoed over to the old-fashioned bureau at the opposite end of the room.

Martha studied her reflection in the mirror above the bureau for fully five minutes. Displeased with her slovenly appearance, she let down her hair and, picking up the comb and hair-brush which Miriam had loaned to Mrs. Nash earlier in the evening, she tried several ways of dressing her hair. Mrs. Nash's gold vanity case next attracted her attention and at least ten minutes were consumed in applying first rouge and then powder. Finally she stood back to note the effect upon her complexion. A slow smile of satisfaction stole across her face, and, without the slightest compunction, she transferred a large gob of the rouge to a piece of tissue paper and, folding it many times, stuffed it inside her dress, for future use.

Tiring of staring at her own countenance, Martha went over to a large bow window and, leaning on the ledge, peered out into the darkness. Familiar as she was with the location of the bedroom, she knew the direction in which she was gazing, but it was impossible for her to distinguish even an outline of the large modern garage which had been built in the rear of the house some years previously. Corbin had told her that he would return from a trip to Upper Marlboro before ten o'clock, but that she was not to wait up for him as he would occupy one of the servants' bedrooms in the garage, the other having been prepared for Pierre, Mrs. Nash's chauffeur.

The weather had moderated with the suddenness which characterizes the disconcerting alterations in temperature in the vicinity of the District of Columbia and southern Maryland. The drip, drip, drip of the thawing snow on the eaves of the house came distinctly to Martha through the half-open window, while the heavy mist, rising from the Patuxent River, on the banks of which the estate of Abbott's Lodge bordered, but made the outer darkness more impenetrable.

With a slight shiver, Martha faced about, thankful for the companionable warmth of the carefully shaded light in the bedroom. It was no night for any one to be out, and for the matter of that, it was time that a hard-working woman was allowed to go to bed. Martha's lips quivered as her grievance increased in importance the more she dwelt upon it. Was she never to be considered? Well, she would go. What was Mrs. Nash to her? The master was dead—

"Paul!"

The name, pronounced with startling distinctness by Mrs. Nash, caused Martha to clutch the window curtains in sudden fright. In the silence that followed she gathered courage to draw closer to the bed. Mrs. Nash lay with eyes tightly closed and Martha judged from her slow and regular breathing that she was still asleep. A hasty glance about the room convinced her that she and Mrs. Nash were alone. Martha crossed herself devoutly just as the sick woman spoke again.

"Paul, can you hear me?" she asked.

Martha's shaking knees carried her only a few inches from the bed, and then curiosity overcame her terror. Mrs. Nash was talking in her sleep. With extreme caution she got down on her hands and knees and crept to the side of the bed. For fully fifteen minutes she crouched there, but Mrs. Nash did not speak again. Slowly and with great pains Martha straightened up sufficiently to get a good look at Mrs. Nash. She had not altered her position and lay with eyes still closed. With the determination of a weak and obstinate nature, Martha decided to remain where she was, and cast about for a satisfactory explanation of her position by the bed should Miriam Ward return. She was laboriously thinking one up when her eyes were attracted by the constant movement of a hand on the pillow. Martha wished most heartily that Mrs. Nash would keep still, and she almost gave tongue to her thoughts; but speech was arrested by the sudden realization that both of Mrs. Nash's hands lay perfectly quiet on the counterpane.

With eyes distended to twice their natural size, Martha watched the third hand slip under the pillow and then out again. As it approached the throat of the sleeping woman, she saw clearly the long, sensitive fingers and the heavy signet ring—

Martha's frayed nerves gave way. Her mouth dropped open and sheer terror gave strength to the shriek which broke from her. When Miriam raced into the room she found her a crumpled, unconscious heap in the center of the floor and Mrs. Nash sitting up in bed regarding her with ashen face.

"Is she dead?" she gasped.

"No; just a faint." Miriam's calm tones belied her feelings; she was almost as startled as Mrs. Nash. "Please lie down again, Mrs. Nash, and keep yourself covered; otherwise you will take cold." She paused by the bedside long enough to pull up the bedclothes and make Mrs. Nash comfortable, then hurried to her emergency kit and from it took a little aromatic spirits of ammonia. Martha revived quickly under the restorative. Later she staggered to her feet and, with Miriam's assistance, took a few halting steps toward the hall door. She stopped abruptly on the threshold at sight of Sheriff Trenholm and Alan waiting anxiously in the hall.

"What has happened?" asked Trenholm. "Is Mrs. Nash worse?"

"No," replied Miriam. "I am not sure what occurred. Martha refuses to tell me. Perhaps if you question her—"

"I felt fainty, like," broke in Martha with marked haste. She avoided looking at the two men. "Please, Miss—Ma'am, take me to my room."

Trenholm read Miriam's hesitation aright. "Go and stay with Mrs. Nash, Alan," he directed, "until Miss Ward returns. Now, Martha," and before the startled housekeeper could protest, he picked her up in his arms and started down the hall. Pausing only long enough to take a bottle of medicine and a glass, Miriam hurried after the sheriff, as Alan went in to speak to Mrs. Nash.

The suite of rooms, comprising sitting room, bedroom and bath, which Corbin and his wife occupied, was at one end of the winding corridor and off a landing halfway up a flight of steps leading to the garret. Miriam took note of the comfortable furniture in the bedroom as she assisted Martha out of her clothes and into bed. The housekeeper was taciturn to the point of sullenness, and Miriam finally forbore to address her.

"Drink this," she handed a glass to Martha as she spoke. "It is a harmless sedative; don't be alarmed," observing the woman's expression. "You will feel better in the morning."

"Will it make me sleep?" asked Martha, huddling down under the blankets.

"Yes." Miriam halted by the door. "Is there anything more I can do for you?"

"No." Martha remembered her manners and her face emerged from under the blankets. "Thank you, Ma'am—Miss. Jest blow out the lamp as you go along."

Miriam hesitated. "You are not afraid to stay in the dark?"

"No, Ma'am—Miss. Good night."

Miriam echoed the words as she carried out Martha's wishes, then closing the door softly she went thoughtfully down the corridor. She had almost reached Mrs. Nash's door when Trenholm called her name softly and joined her a moment later.

"Did you learn anything from the housekeeper?" he asked.

She shook her head. "Martha hardly spoke." Miriam paused. "Her condition may be due to hysteria."

Trenholm studied her expression. "But you don't think so—"

She looked straight at him. "No. I believe the woman was almost paralyzed with fright."

Trenholm remained silent for a few seconds, then roused himself.

"You may be right," he said. "I hope Mrs. Nash suffers no ill effects from her rude awakening. A moment, Miss Ward," as Miriam laid her hand on Mrs. Nash's bedroom door. "Please tell Mr. Mason that I will remain with Abbott's body. If you," he lowered his voice almost to a whisper, "if you need me, you will find me there," and turning he went down the corridor.

Alan Mason rose at Miriam's approach and relinquished his seat by the bedside, with a relieved air.

"Mrs. Nash *will* talk," he remarked, "although I tried to monopolize the conversation in the hope of making her sleepy. Is there anything more I can do?" His question was intended for Miriam but Mrs. Nash answered it.

"Close the door behind you," she said tartly, and Alan colored as he met Miriam's dark eyes, with a faint quizzical gleam in them.

"Sheriff Trenholm is with the body," she murmured, as he passed her on his way out of the room. "Good night."

"What did you say?" demanded Mrs. Nash, raising herself on her elbow.

Miriam bent over her and straightened the pillows with a practiced hand. "Isn't that more comfortable?" she asked, as Mrs. Nash sank back with a sigh. "It is time for your medicine," glancing, as she spoke, at her wrist watch. "Just a second," and moving swiftly over to the table, she prepared it and then returned to the bed. She expected some difficulty in persuading Mrs. Nash to take it, but to her secret surprise the latter swallowed it without a murmur, but with a wry face.

"Roberts never prescribed an agreeable dose," she commented, after sipping a glass of water. "Sit by me, Miss Ward, I want to ask you some questions."

"Not to-night," Miriam's charming smile softened her refusal. "You must go to sleep."

"With that howl still ringing in my ears!" Mrs. Nash's shudder was no affectation, but a true indication of her state of mind. "What possessed the woman?"

"Hysterics," briefly. "Now, Mrs. Nash, you really must close your eyes."

"In a minute. Sit down just a second." Mrs. Nash's tone could be coaxing when she wished. "I'll do whatever you say if you will answer a few questions."

"I can't promise."

"Now, don't be obstinate." Mrs. Nash glanced at her shrewdly. "If you irritate me, I'll not sleep at all," and she squared her shoulders with an air of determination which made Miriam's heart sink. She knew, none better, that often temper and temperature went hand and hand in the sick room. Humoring a patient was occasionally a short cut to health as well as peace.

"What is it you wish to know?" she asked, sitting down.

Mrs. Nash smiled, well pleased with having gained her point.

"What killed Paul?" she asked, and at Miriam's frown, added hastily: "There is nothing in that question to send my temperature skyward. Was he poisoned?"

"No; stabbed." Miriam met her piercing black eyes steadily, while wondering at the concentration of her regard. Mrs. Nash sat bolt upright.

"Was the knife left in the body?" she demanded.

"No."

"Have they found it?"

"No." Miriam hastened to supplement her second monosyllable with a further statement as she saw another question trembling on Mrs. Nash's lips. "The weapon has not been found *yet*."

"Then how do they know that he was stabbed?" persisted Mrs. Nash.

"By the nature of the wound," replied Miriam. "Sheriff Trenholm told me just now that the autopsy proved Mr. Abbott died from what is known as a punctured wound."

"And what is that precisely?"

"Why, the weapon used left a fusiform or spindle-shaped wound," she added, observing Mrs. Nash's blank expression. "Now, please lie down again, for that is the last question I am going to answer to-night," and the gentle firmness of her voice convinced Mrs. Nash that she meant what she said. But before she settled back on the pillows she looked around at her nurse.

"Was my niece talking to Guy Trenholm in the hall before you came in here a second time?" she inquired.

Miriam shook her head in the negative. "Not to my knowledge. I have not seen Miss Carter since dinner."

Mrs. Nash grunted as she turned over on her side. "Well, if Betty slept through Martha's dreadful scream she rivals the seven sleepers," she commented and closed her eyes.

It was after three o'clock when Miriam threw back the blanket which she had wrapped around herself and rose softly from the chair by the bedside. Mrs. Nash had been asleep for fully two hours. Miriam was thoroughly chilled and she chafed one hand over the other as she walked noiselessly up and down the bedroom, hoping to stimulate circulation. She stopped finally by the table where stood the lamp and laid her hands on its glass globe. As she stood warming them by the heat from the lamp, she observed a bowl of nuts pushed toward the back of the table. Her vigil had sharpened her appetite, and she had regretted several times that she had neglected to ask Martha for a night lunch.

Reaching over she pulled the bowl toward her and took up one of the walnuts and the nut cracker. As the instrument crunched over the nut, it sounded in the stillness like a miniature firecracker and she paused, and looked over her shoulder in alarm at her patient. Apparently the noise had not disturbed Mrs. Nash, for she slept peacefully on. Several tempting pieces of the nut meat stuck in the shell and not daring to use the nut cracker again, she started to take up the nut pick lying in the bowl. For fully five seconds she stood staring at it, her hand poised in mid-air; then with one hurried, comprehensive look about the room and at her sleeping patient, she picked up the bowl and sped into the hall, her flying footsteps deadened by the strip of carpet which ran its length, and brought up breathless by the sofa on which Sheriff Trenholm had thrown himself, fully dressed, a short time before.

"Look!" she exclaimed, keeping her voice lowered in spite of her excitement, and she pointed to the nut pick. It was of finest steel, about eight inches long, with a straight, sharp point and sharpened fluted edges running along its sides. From point to handle it was stained a dull red.

"Blood!" The word escaped Guy Trenholm in little more than a whisper, and simultaneously they turned to the undertaker's couch near the center of the room on which lay all that was mortal of Paul Abbott.

"The wound was spindle-shaped," Miriam added in a voice not quite steady, and Trenholm bowed his head.

"You have found the weapon, undoubtedly," he said. "Thank you."

CHAPTER VII
CURIOUS QUESTIONS AND EVASIVE ANSWERS

DOCTOR ROBERTS laid down his stethoscope and frowned as he gazed at Mrs. Nash, lying back on her pillow, both eyes closed, and breathing rapidly. Leaning forward he picked up her chart and read Miriam's notations on it with a wrinkled brow.

"You must stay in bed another day," he said finally. "The flu is treacherous."

Mrs. Nash's eyes slowly opened and regarded him steadily. "What's the matter with your medicines?" she demanded. "Why am I not better?"

"Don't be so impatient." He evaded a direct reply. "Where is Miss Ward?"

"Asleep, I presume. She went to her room after giving me my breakfast this morning." Mrs. Nash sat up a little straighter. "Where did you find such a pretty woman?"

"She came from the Central Registry; I know no more than that." Roberts looked at her inquiringly. "You find her competent and intelligent?"

"As nurses go." Mrs. Nash sniffed. An argument with Miriam that morning, in which she had come off second best, still rankled. "I admit that she is nicer in the sick room than my niece Betty."

"Has Betty been with you this morning?"

"Yes," grimly. "She was worse than useless. Well," regarding Roberts attentively, "why, do you look at me like that?"

"Betty is hardly herself, Mrs. Nash, since the tragedy of yesterday."

Mrs. Nash did not give him time to complete his sentence. "So you, too, think Betty is crushed? Well, so she is—on some one else."

"My dear Mrs. Nash!"

Mrs. Nash smiled tolerantly and swiftly changed the subject.

"Who were all those people tramping by my door a short time ago?" she asked.

"The coroner's jury," responded Roberts, putting his stethoscope and sphygmomanometer in his bag.

"Oh!" Mrs. Nash sat upright; her cheeks a brighter pink. "Is the inquest being held here?"

"Not now. It met, was sworn in, and viewed the body," replied Roberts concisely. "And then Coroner Dixon asked for a postponement—"

"Why, for goodness' sakes!" demanded Mrs. Nash. "Doesn't the man wish to catch Paul's murderer?"

"Of course he does!" Roberts was conscious of a feeling of irritation; Mrs. Nash's interminable questions were getting on his nerves. "Sheriff Trenholm wished more time before presenting the case, and the inquest is held over for a few days."

"Does that mean that the burial has to be postponed?" she asked.

Roberts shook his head. "The body will be removed to the vault at the cemetery," he answered. "I do not know what arrangements Alan Mason has made, further than that. Now, Mrs. Nash, you must not excite yourself," observing her flushed appearance with concern. "Please lie down."

Mrs. Nash subsided among the pillows, of which she had collected four, arranged entirely to her liking after earnest effort on Martha's part to carry out her orders.

"Will you do me a favor, Doctor?" she asked as he rose and stood, bag in hand. "Please give this note to Pierre, my chauffeur, and tell him to drive into Washington and give it to my husband. Pierre is to return here immediately with every article listed in the note. If I must stay here, I will at least be comfortable."

Roberts took the proffered note. "I will run in and see you to-night before returning to Washington," he volunteered. "Sheriff Trenholm has asked me to dine with him."

Mrs. Nash raised her head. "I recall Paul's father speaking to me some years ago about a young man in whom he was interested. His name was Guy Trenholm."

"It is the same person," declared Roberts. "Trenholm owes much to Abbott's generosity; he practically educated him. Now, Mrs. Nash, be sure and take the medicine prescribed, and, above all, mind what the nurse tells you." He chuckled at her disgusted expression and, with a graceful bow, left the room.

But Roberts had ceased smiling when he went down the staircase and out of the house. Mrs. Nash's condition puzzled him. He had been her family physician ever since her father, Owen Carter, the senior Congressman from his state, had taken up his residence in Washington. A woman spoiled, self-willed, she had held undisputed sway in her father's household, while her frail mother had been content with the role of invalid. Mrs. Nash had allowed her eccentricities to grow upon her and Washington society had enjoyed many a quiet laugh at her expense. Her social position, her wealth, as well as her undoubted good looks and her quick wit, made her a welcome visitor. Rumors of her approaching marriage with this dignitary and that had been frequently circulated, in spite of her declaration that she preferred to be an old maid. Her marriage, therefore, to the Reverend Alexander Nash had proved something of a sensation in their small world. That her ambitions had been satisfied on becoming the wife of an unknown Doctor of Divinity, her friends and acquaintances found hard to believe.

Roberts went down the path immersed in thought. In a telephone talk that morning, Representative Carter had expressed great anxiety about his daughter's condition and begged the doctor to see her again and curb her imprudent tendencies to neglect her health. Thereupon Roberts had turned over his patients in Washington to his assistant and motored out to Abbott's Lodge. A cause for wonderment, which persisted even after his talk with Mrs. Nash, was why her father had shown such anxiety about her and not her husband.

Roberts was still pondering deeply when he reached the garage and Pierre's respectful, "*Bonjour*, Monsieur," brought him back to his errand.

"Morning, Pierre," he replied. "Mrs. Nash wishes you to run into Washington with this note for her husband."

Pierre wiped his fingers on some waste and taking the white envelope gingerly, tucked it in the pocket of his jumper.

"Yes, Monsieur, and when shall I start?"

"Now, I suppose. Have you lunched?"

"Mrs. Corbin gave me some sandwiches and tea." Pierre picked up his chamois and can of metal polish. "That car of yours, Monsieur, it is good, but it has a slapping piston."

"Impossible!" Roberts went over to his roadster and lifted the hood. The car was a new investment and his pride. "It was the pump you heard, Pierre, and not a piston."

"Perhaps, Monsieur," Pierre's shrug was characteristic. "Allow me," and with a quick turn of his supple wrists, he fastened the hood back in place. "But when you next start your engine, listen well."

"Thanks, I will," Roberts started to enter his car when the chauffeur addressed him again, somewhat diffidently.

"Please, Monsieur, is Madame very ill?" he asked.

"She fears she has the flu," replied Roberts. "But there is nothing alarming about her condition, Pierre."

"Is she better than last night?"

"Yes." At the servant's persistency Roberts closed the door of his car without entering it and regarded the little chauffeur keenly. A thought struck him. There was a perceptible pause before he again spoke. "When did Doctor Nash return to Washington?"

"Monday night we got in, Monsieur." Pierre paused to calculate on his fingers. "That is, Tuesday morning."

"Ah, then you came down on a night train from New York?"

"But, no, Monsieur. Doctor Nash and Miss Carter leave me on the train at Baltimore on Monday afternoon, and the doctor he reach home on Tuesday morning."

Roberts' glance at Pierre became a stare. "And Miss Carter?" he questioned quickly.

A shrug of Pierre's shoulders was most expressive. "I know nothing, Monsieur. I leave the house early to go to the garage and put Madame's car in order." Swiftly he changed the subject. "Does Madame wish me to come back from Washington to-night?"

"Yes, and I imagine from what she said, that Mrs. Nash will be impatient for your return," replied Roberts, going toward the door. "Report to the nurse when you reach here."

"*Oui*, Monsieur." Pierre touched his forehead with his finger, then as Roberts disappeared up the walk he turned and stared at his reflection in the polished surface of the Rolls-Royce. His little pig eyes were keenly alert and he flecked an infinitesimal speck of dirt from the car door before turning away and going to his room on the floor above.

"I am to see the nurse," he muttered below his breath. "*Eh bien*—perhaps!"

Most of the snow had melted in the sudden thaw of the night before and a comparatively mild temperature and brilliant sunlight tempted Roberts to stay out of doors. Turning about he strode briskly away from the house. He had traversed half the distance to the Patuxent River when he caught sight of a woman approaching along the path. Her quick, buoyant step and fine carriage first attracted his attention, and as she drew nearer he recognized Miriam Ward. At sight of him she hastened her footsteps.

"Good afternoon, Doctor," she exclaimed. "Have you seen Mrs. Nash?"

"I have just come from her bedroom," he answered. "When do you go on duty, Miss Ward?"

"This evening," Miriam responded. "I left her after breakfast. Mrs. Nash prefers to have me do night duty. How did you find her?"

"Her general condition is better, but frankly, there are certain symptoms that puzzle me," admitted Roberts. "I noticed by your chart that she had a subnormal temperature this morning. Her temperature is still down, her pulse sluggish, and respiration rapid."

"She insists that she has the flu," Miriam pointed out. "But the symptoms are contradictory."

"True." Roberts adjusted his eyeglasses. "That is what puzzles me. I have made a careful examination and find both lungs are clear. I feel that I have not located the real trouble."

"You don't consider her able to sit up out of bed?" questioned Miriam. "I ask because she insists upon doing so."

"Most certainly not," promptly. "The old house is full of draughts and improperly heated, and there might be danger of pneumonia in her run-down condition. I left a few directions on the chart for you," added Roberts; then as Miriam, with a slight bow, started to walk past him toward the house, he detained her with a gesture. "Was the clergyman, who accompanied Miss Carter on Monday night to Abbott's sick room, her aunt's husband, the Reverend Doctor Nash?"

At the direct question Miriam's color rose. "I am not sure of the relationship," she replied. "But to the best of my recollection, he certainly mentioned that his name was Nash."

In silence Roberts fingered his hat which he had not replaced on his head since stopping to speak to Miriam.

"And Betty Carter denied that she had visited Paul," he muttered. "It is most singular!"

He echoed Miriam's thoughts, but she forbore to comment. Taking a mere acquaintance into her confidence was foreign to her reserved nature. Suddenly Roberts turned to her, his fine eyes twinkling with one of his rare smiles.

"I admire your discretion," he said. "If I can be of any service at any time call upon me," and with a friendly wave of his hand, he continued his interrupted stroll toward the river.

As Miriam approached the house she walked more slowly. Her hour in the fresh, invigorating air had done her more good than any tonic, and her long, uninterrupted sleep that morning had refreshed her. It was her first walk about the grounds since coming to Abbott's Lodge, and she had admired the scenery and well-kept appearance of the estate. For the first time she realized the size of the house as she went around the path that skirted it; it was far larger than she had supposed. Entering through the sunparlor, she halted in the dining room at sight of Sheriff Trenholm conversing with Charles Corbin, the caretaker.

Trenholm's attention was diverted from Corbin by the nurse's arrival, and the caretaker seized the chance to edge his portly form nearer the pantry door. He stopped abruptly as the sheriff's hawklike gaze turned swiftly back to him, and rubbed the back of his hand across his dry lips.

"Don't go, Miss Ward," exclaimed Trenholm. "You have come most opportunely. Exactly where did you find the bowl of nuts last night?"

"Standing on the small lamp table in the room now occupied by Mrs. Nash," she replied. "It was pushed back against the wall."

"When did you take that nut dish there, Corbin?" Trenholm stepped closer as he put the question and the caretaker wriggled his shoulders against the wall; the support brought back his lost sense of security. He had no love for the sheriff of the county.

"Mr. Abbott brought the nuts in some time last week," he retorted. "I disremember the exact day, but he poured them in a bowl that usually sits over yonder on the sideboard, and he took it away—I don't know where."

"Think again, Corbin," cautioned Trenholm as the man moved uneasily. "When did you last see that bowl and the nut pick?"

"I told you I can't think of the exact day," was the surly reply. An idea occurred to him and his parchment-like face brightened. "I'll get Martha; she'll know."

"Wait!" Trenholm's voice rang out clearly and Corbin stopped where he was. "I'll talk to your wife later. Who used Mrs. Nash's bedroom?"

"It was Mr. Abbott's bedroom, and after his death it was closed," answered Corbin. "But lately Mr. Paul has used it as a sitting room. He told Martha it made him feel that his father was nearby and he wasn't so lonesome."

Trenholm viewed the caretaker in silence for a moment. "So Mr. Paul used to sit there, did he?" he asked, and Corbin contented himself with a sullen nod of his closely shaven, bullet-shaped head. "And when were you last in the room?"

"This morning." Corbin dropped his eyes that Trenholm might not read their expression of relief at the change in the trend of his questions. "I went in to make up the fire for Mrs. Nash. There's the telephone, sir."

"I'll answer it," and turning on his heel Trenholm hastened into the living room and over to the telephone.

In an instant Corbin was gone and Miriam almost rubbed her eyes, so swift were his movements and so noiseless. Pausing long enough to pour herself out a glass of water and drink it, she followed Trenholm into the living room. The sheriff was still at the telephone and she walked over to Paul Abbott's desk and sat down before it, intending to wait until Trenholm was disengaged.

Miriam was idly playing with one of the silver desk ornaments when she saw a package of envelopes lying on the edge of an open leather bag, which stood on a stool by the desk. Near at hand was an empty scrap basket. Again Miriam's gaze sought the envelopes. They were oddly familiar. Stooping forward she took up the package and fingered them. In quality of paper, in quantity of stamps, they matched the half-burnt envelope which she had picked up in her bedroom twenty-four hours before. Her envelope was securely locked in her grip, but she vividly remembered the Canadian postage stamps, orange in color and five in number.

Miriam looked across the room at Guy Trenholm. He was still talking at the telephone with his back turned to her. She was oblivious of the fact that she was distinctly visible to him in the mirror hanging just before him on the wall.

Miriam studied the handwriting on the topmost envelope—it bore Paul Abbott's name and address. Swiftly she examined the address on each envelope—it was the same—then counted them—eleven in all. Miriam's thoughts reverted to the black crest on her torn envelope. She turned over the eleven envelopes—the flap on each was missing.

"Miss Ward." Betty Carter's voice just over her shoulder made her start violently. "Will you go to my aunt at once; she needs you."

"Certainly." Miriam was conscious of Betty's cold regard; but there was no hurry discernible in her movements as she replaced the rubber band around the envelopes and laid them back on the top of the open bag, which, she noticed for the first time, bore, stamped upon it, Guy Trenholm's initials.

CHAPTER VIII
BLACKMAIL

BETTY CARTER watched Miriam disappear up the staircase before she moved. Crossing the living room she stopped in front of the fire and warmed her hands, then sitting down she toyed idly with a string of pearls about her neck.

"Still conscious of your pearls?" asked Guy Trenholm. He had followed her across the room and paused in front of her.

Betty crimsoned from neck to brow and her eyes flamed with wrath.

"If you can't refrain from insults, don't address me," she said.

It was Trenholm's turn to color. "You misunderstood me," he exclaimed. "Seeing you playing with your pearls reminded me of your inordinate fondness for jewelry when in Paris."

"Inordinate fondness," echoed Betty, and her delicately arched eyebrows rose in displeasure. "Your explanation is in as questionable taste as your first remark."

Trenholm shrugged his shoulders. "If you take offense so easily, we'll change the subject," he said. "Where were you off to so early this morning?"

She looked at him without speaking and Trenholm occupied the time in lighting a cigarette, after first asking her permission, which was given with a nod of her head.

When she finally spoke it was to ask a question and not to answer his.

"I cannot understand," she began, "why a man of your capabilities accepted the office of sheriff. Have you no ambition to make good in the future?"

"The future?" his smile was bitter. "The future can take care of itself. What concerns me is the present. Where did Pierre take you in your aunt's car before breakfast this morning?"

Her lips curled in a disdainful smile. "If you wish to know, why not question Pierre?"

"Because I prefer to come to you rather than ask a servant," he stated quietly. "Take your time, I'll wait for an answer," and he dropped into a chair by the side of the big sofa on which she was sitting.

"I see, patience is a virtue with you," she remarked. "Is it, by chance, your only virtue?"

He shrugged his broad shoulders. "Time will tell." A glint of humor lit his deep-set eyes. She met his look for a second, then glanced away.

Through the drifting smoke of his cigarette Trenholm studied her intently; her beauty was undeniable and of an unusual type. He sighed. Was the droop at the corners of her mouth indicative of deceit? Was it in her to play straight?

Betty moved restlessly, suddenly conscious of his prolonged scrutiny. "Suppose I tell you that I went to early church in Upper Marlboro," she said suddenly.

"On Wednesday?"

"Certainly. One can pray on any day."

"And not necessarily in a church."

Betty snuggled down more comfortably among the cushions, but one hand, tucked carefully out of sight, was tightly clenched. "So you still sneer at religion," she commented softly.

Trenholm shook his head. "I would never scoff did I for one instant believe that true religion has a part in your life." At his answer her eyes sparkled with anger, but she masked her feelings under an ingratiating smile.

"You have changed, Guy Trenholm, since the old days in France," she remarked, and her voice held an undertone of feeling he failed to understand.

"For the worse?" he asked quickly.

"Perhaps." She lapsed into silence, which he did not care to break. His air of strength, of self-sufficiency, irritated her and she watched him covertly while pretending to be absorbed in thought. Even her fastidious taste could find no fault with his well-tailored riding suit and leather boots. She grudgingly admitted to herself that the years had brought improvement in raiment if not in manners. Whatever else he became, he would never be metamorphosed into a society man. No social badinage would cover his thoughts; he would say what he had to say with sledge-hammer effect whatever the occasion. Betty's heavy sigh was audible and he glanced at her inquiringly.

"Strange, is it not," he began, as she remained silent, "that you and Alan and I should be thrown together as we were in France during the War, and that we should meet under Paul's roof."

"Not so very remarkable," she objected. "We have seen each other frequently during the past five years."

Trenholm threw his cigarette into the fire and leaned forward.

"What motive inspired Paul's murder?" he asked.

His question robbed her cheeks of color. "Why ask me that?" she demanded. "Why should I know more than another?"

"Because Paul loved you."

Her lips twitched and her eyes grew dim. She put up her hand as if to ward off a blow. "Don't!" She recovered her poise, shaken for a fraction of a second. "I refuse to discuss Paul's death with you, of all men."

Trenholm considered her, slowly, carefully, as he leaned back in his chair. "Other men loved you," he said softly. "I, for one."

"In Paris?"

"Yes," quietly. He pressed his lips together. "Calf love—I got over it."

Betty laughed not quite steadily. "You are to be congratulated." She spoke with a mockery and malice so neatly balanced that for a swift second he failed to reply.

"I recovered," he stated, more forcefully. "Others didn't." His glance held hers. "Paul is dead, but Alan Mason still lives in his fool's paradise."

With one spring she gained her feet and faced him, trembling with rage and excitement.

"After all, Guy Trenholm, the role of sheriff becomes you," she said, and the scorn in her voice stung him. "Water seeks its own level." She turned away, snatched her coat from a chair where she had left it that morning and swung out of the door.

Trenholm sat where he was for fully five minutes after the front door had closed behind Betty. When he rose he was still frowning. Going over to his bag he tossed the package of letters inside, snapped the bag to, locked it, and taking up his cap went in search of Martha Corbin.

Betty was unconscious of the distance she walked or the direction she took. She was grateful for the cool breeze that fanned her hot cheeks. Seldom had she felt in such a fever; her throat was dry—parched. She paused long enough to wipe tiny beads of moisture from her forehead with an already damp handkerchief. She had spent the night in choking back sobs which racked her slender body. Toward morning she had slept fitfully from pure exhaustion. Only a relentless purpose spurred her to get up, regardless of the early hour, a purpose frustrated by—

Betty drew in a long breath and let it out slowly. She stopped and gazed about for a familiar landmark. She knew the countryside fairly well, and it did not take her long to locate the road which led to Upper Marlboro. She found it drier walking on its crest and trudged slowly along, keeping a wary eye out for automobiles which would make necessary a hasty run for the side of the road. She judged that she had covered about half the distance when, in passing a wood which she remembered was located on Abbott's property, she saw a man running through the trees in her direction. Something furtive in his movements as he dodged among the leafless trees and bushes caused her heart to beat more rapidly, and she cast a glance behind her. No vehicle, horse-drawn or motor-driven, was in sight. Betty faltered and came to a stop, then, throwing off her unreasoning fear, she hurried forward, glancing neither to the right nor the left.

Betty had passed the wood and was breathing more easily when she detected the sound of following footsteps and she heard her name called once, and then again with more insistence. She kept straight ahead, for if recollection did not play her false, a farmhouse was around the next bend in the road. She had almost gained the turn, when a man's shadow was thrown on the snow just in front of her, and facing to her left she found Charles Corbin, the caretaker, at her side.

"Excuse me, Miss Betty," he said, with a tug at the visor of his cap. "I thought ye heard me coming."

Betty's feeling of relief found vent in a slight laugh. "Dear me, Corbin; I wish I had recognized you sooner. Why, I was actually running away from you."

Corbin's parchment-like face opened in an expansive grin which showed his yellow teeth. "Running away, was you, Miss Betty?" His voice dropped to a confidential pitch. "Take it from me, don't ye do it."

Betty ceased laughing with startling abruptness and stared at him.

"What are you talking about, Corbin?" she demanded.

His right eye opened and closed in a most expressive wink. "I want to speak to ye, Miss Betty, confidential like."

"Well?" she drew back and looked at him in dawning comprehension. "Are you drunk?"

"No; I never touch liquor." He slipped his hand inside his tightly buttoned coat and drew out a woman's silk scarf and held it just beyond her reach.

"Where did you get that?" she cried.

"Where ye dropped it the morning of Mr. Paul's murder." As he spoke he shook out the scarf. "The blood's still on it," and he leered at her as she raised her eyes and looked at him. It was some seconds before she spoke, and her voice was not quite natural.

"Well, what's your price?" she asked.

Corbin licked his lips. "How much ye got with ye?" he demanded.

From an inside pocket she drew out a bill folder containing "A.B.A." travelers' checks. Only one was left, but tucked behind it were two yellow-back Treasury notes.

"I can give you a check for fifty dollars or these two twenty-dollar bills," she explained.

"I'll take the money—on account."

The look she gave him was expressive of her feelings, but wasted on Corbin. "Very well," she said. "Hand me the scarf."

"Oh, no." He held it behind him. "Not till I get five hundred dollars."

"Five hundred dollars!"

"Sure—that's what Sheriff Trenholm will give for it and, eh, other information."

Betty threw back her head and eyed him defiantly. "If you go to the sheriff he will give you what every blackmailer deserves—nothing." And she replaced the bills in the check folder. Corbin eyed the vanishing money in alarm.

"Don't be in a hurry!" he exclaimed. "I am a poor man. I'll take the money—and your word for the rest." His fingers closed greedily over the Treasury notes as he relinquished the scarf. With a mumbled word, of which Betty was oblivious, he hastened back the way he had come.

Betty stood where she was in indecision. Finally she turned and watched Corbin reënter the woods. Convinced that he was not likely to return she continued on her way toward Upper Marlboro, the scarf safely tucked inside the pocket of her fur coat. She had gone some little distance when she came to an open field and saw, close to the road, in a slight hollow, a huge boulder from which the snow had melted, leaving exposed the dry rock.

Betty's hesitation was brief. Climbing the fence, she turned her back on the road and placing the scarf on the rock she drew out a silver match box. The first match failed to light, with the second she was more successful, and three minutes later the scarf was a smoldering heap of ashes. Drawing in her breath she blew them off the rock, and with a lighter heart, regained the road just in time to recognize her aunt's Rolls-Royce approaching, Pierre at the wheel. The recognition was mutual and the powerful car came to a stop. Before the little chauffeur could climb out of his seat the limousine door was swung open and Doctor Nash sprang to Betty's side, and assisted her into the car.

"Upon my word, Betty!" he exclaimed, at her wet boots. "You are most imprudent!"

"As usual." A sigh accompanied the words and Doctor Nash turned and scanned her closely. Her brilliant color and the sparkle of her eyes accentuated the haggard lines caused by harassing thoughts and sleepless nights, but did not detract from her beauty. Nash's critical expression softened and Betty, quick to read his thoughts, laid her hand in his. "I need your help."

"You can count on me, Betty, always." Nash spoke with warmth and Betty's color deepened. She paused, however, before addressing him again.

"Promise me," she began, sinking her voice so that he had to bend nearer to catch what she said. "Promise me not to admit to Sheriff Trenholm that you and I were at Abbott's Lodge on Monday night."

Nash straightened up with a jerk. "Betty!"

"Please!" Betty's soft voice was pathos itself. There was silence in the limousine and Pierre dropped his eyes from the vision mirror in which were plainly outlined the likenesses of his two passengers in time to turn into the driveway to Abbott's Lodge and stop under the *porte cochère*.

Nash sighed deeply. "Does your aunt know?"

Betty shook her head. "No one must know," she protested vehemently. "*No one.*" She looked at him and the wistful, pleading appeal in her lovely eyes stirred him out of himself.

His low but fervid "Betty" reached not only her ears, but Alan Mason's, who stood by the door of the car, held open by the attentive Pierre.

Alan broke the pause. "I'm glad you've come, Nash," he said. "Your wife is worse."

CHAPTER IX
THE DENIAL

DOCTOR ROBERTS removed his fingers from Mrs. Nash's wrist, after taking her pulse, and then bowed gravely to her husband.

"Your wife has rallied and we can safely leave her with the nurse," he said. "Come, Nash, you must be very weary after your anxious night," and laying his hand persuasively on his companion's shoulder he gently pushed him toward the hall door, then turned back to speak to Miriam. "I will be downstairs in the living room if you need me."

Miriam, in the act of preparing Mrs. Nash's medicine, did not answer. Going over to the bed she aroused the drowsy woman, helped her to a sitting position and held the medicine glass to her lips. Mrs. Nash drank slowly, and then settled back with a low sigh. Miriam busied herself about the bedroom for ten minutes before returning to the chair by the bed and found her patient regarding her steadfastly.

"When did my husband get here?" she asked.

"Around six o'clock yesterday afternoon," replied Miriam.

"I do not remember." Mrs. Nash passed her hand before her eyes. "He came while I was unconscious—?"

"Yes. Now, Mrs. Nash, don't talk—"

"Was he with me all night?" Paying no attention to Miriam, she struggled up on her elbow as she put the question.

"He was in and out of the room most of the night," Miriam bent over and adjusted the bedclothes. "Doctor Roberts was here also."

Mrs. Nash was silent for some little time, her eyes roving about the big room, into which the daylight was stealing through the partly open windows; finally she gazed again at her nurse.

"I wasn't so ill that I could not appreciate what you did for me," she said, and Miriam was surprised at the amount of feeling in her voice. "I shan't forget it, my dear."

"Indeed, Mrs. Nash, you must not excite yourself," Miriam protested, coloring warmly at her praise. "Please lie down again and try to sleep."

"How about you?" with a keen glance at her. "Have you had any sleep? Ah, I can see you haven't, so don't lie." The injunction slipped out with Mrs. Nash's customary abruptness and Miriam could not forbear a smile.

Undoubtedly Mrs. Nash was recovering. "Go and lie down on that cot which I had Martha bring here yesterday afternoon for you. Don't be afraid"—with a fleeting smile—"I'll make my wants known." And considering the argument settled Mrs. Nash turned to a more comfortable position and closed her eyes.

Without moving Miriam considered her in silence. It was only when she heard Mrs. Nash's regular breathing and realized that she had fallen into peaceful slumber that she walked over to the cot and, drawing back the heavy blanket, threw herself, dressed as she was, down upon it. Her head had hardly touched the pillow before she was sound asleep. An hour passed and she still slept on, totally unaware that some one had stealthily entered the room.

Mrs. Nash stirred, opened her eyes and sat up. What was the noise which had awakened her? Her eyes darted about the room as she turned her head from side to side, and she bent this way and that to get a better view of each piece of furniture. A gentle snore from Miriam suggested a solution—had a louder snore aroused her? Mrs. Nash lay back among the pillows, but she did not close her eyes.

It was close upon eight o'clock when Miriam awoke and, refreshed by her long nap, sprang up, to find Mrs. Nash's bright black eyes regarding her with an expression she could not fathom.

The desultory conversation about the breakfast table ceased altogether with the departure into the pantry of Anna, the capable daughter of a neighboring farmer, whom Martha had secured to aid her in caring for the guests at Abbott's Lodge. She had often assisted Martha when Paul Abbott and his father had entertained parties in the hunting season and her familiarity with the household arrangements made her presence invaluable at the moment to the overworked housekeeper, whose duties had multiplied with the alarming illness of Mrs. Nash.

Doctor Roberts and Alan Mason had eaten with relish Martha's buckwheat cakes and country sausage, but Alexander Nash scarcely tasted a mouthful of the appetizing breakfast, contenting himself with several cups of black coffee.

"Must you return to Washington, Roberts?" he asked, pushing aside his plate.

"Yes; I must be at Garfield by noon for an important operation." Roberts paused to light a cigar handed to him by Alan. "There is every reason to believe that Mrs. Nash will continue to improve."

Nash looked moodily at the unused knife which he was balancing between his fingers. "Is there any country doctor in the neighborhood, Alan, whom we could call on in an emergency?" he asked.

"I suppose so," Alan stopped to knock the ashes from his cigar into his coffee cup. "I'll get in touch with Trenholm and ask him."

"Hold on," exclaimed Roberts, as Alan pushed back his chair, preparatory to rising. "I don't know, Nash, how competent the country doctors are, but you can safely trust Miss Ward should another crisis arise."

"The nurse?" The question was put by Nash with raised eyebrows, and Roberts frowned. He did not relish the clergyman's tone.

"The nurse," he repeated, with dry emphasis. "But for her keeping her wits about her Mrs. Nash would have died yesterday afternoon, before I could get to her."

"What was the cause of my wife's critical condition?" asked Nash. "You have never told me."

"Heart collapse," tersely. "Miss Ward's prompt use of camphorated oil, administered hypodermically, brought her around, however, and her clever nursing has aided materially in her recovery from the attack. Come, Nash, don't be so downhearted; you can place every confidence in Miss Ward."

Nash laid down his napkin. "I'll be more easy in my mind if you will return," he admitted. "Miss Ward is undoubtedly clever, but, at that, only a nurse—"

"A damned fine looking one!" ejaculated Alan, emerging from behind a screen of tobacco smoke. "Come, Nash, why have you taken such a prejudice against her?"

Nash glanced angrily at the younger man, but refrained from a direct answer.

"Suppose we drop the discussion," he said. "I will be greatly obliged, Roberts, if you will promise to get back later to-day."

"I will try," was Roberts' noncommittal reply. "It depends upon how I find my patients and my assistant's report whether I can spend to-night here. I will run up now and see Mrs. Nash," and not waiting to hear anything further, he left the dining room.

As Roberts reached the second floor, Miriam rose from her seat in the alcove, where she had been eating her breakfast, and accompanied him into the sick room. Mrs. Nash, with Martha sitting watchfully by the bed, was dozing, and Roberts refrained from arousing her. Once again in the hall he paused to speak to Miriam before going down the stairs.

"Keep up the same treatment," he directed. "Do not let her exert herself in any way, and no excitement, mind—"

Miriam hesitated. "Is she to see any one?" she asked.

"I leave that to your discretion." He paused for thought. "Don't permit any discussion—any arguments." He came back a step. "I wouldn't let her mind dwell too much on Mr. Abbott's murder, and discourage her from talking about it."

"I do, Doctor." Miriam looked down the empty hall, and then back at Roberts. "Don't you think you had better get a second nurse?"

"That's not necessary now," exclaimed Roberts. "In fact, two nurses would alarm Mrs. Nash unduly about her condition. You are getting some sleep, aren't you?"

"Yes. I'm supposed to be off duty now, but I don't like to leave her."

"Oh, have Martha alternate with Miss Carter in the sick room; they can call you if she has another attack." He noticed her change in expression, and, struck by an idea, asked in a lower voice: "Are Mrs. Nash and her niece on good terms?"

"Why, yes," glancing at him in surprise, and Roberts looked sharply at her.

"Sure?"

"Certainly; I have seen nothing to make me think otherwise," with more insistence, as he still looked dubious.

"Where is Miss Carter now?"

"Breakfasting in her room, Martha told me. She has volunteered to spend the morning with her aunt, and—"

"Then you must go to your room and rest." Roberts started down the staircase. "I have promised Nash to return to-night. If an emergency arises, you have my telephone number," and the busy physician hurried away just as Martha appeared in Mrs. Nash's doorway.

"Please, Miss—Ma'am," she came further into the hall at sight of Miriam. "Mrs. Nash is sleeping nicely. Can I get Miss Betty to come to her aunt?"

"Surely, Martha," but the housekeeper still hung back, instead of going on her errand, and she added, "What is it?"

Martha came nearer and lowered her voice.

"Before she fell asleep she said to tell you to ask her husband to send for her maid, Somers, to come and help take care of her," and her message delivered in one breathless sentence, Martha went down the hall to Betty's bedroom.

Miriam went thoughtfully over to the alcove and arranged the soiled dishes on her breakfast tray while she considered Mrs. Nash's message. If Somers was the right kind of person she would be invaluable. Martha's white face, and nervous, excitable manner pointed inevitably to one conclusion—Martha's usefulness as a nurse's aid would soon be a thing of the past, indeed, if indications could be depended upon, she might become a patient herself; for to Miriam's practiced eye, the housekeeper was on the verge of a nervous collapse.

From where she stood in the window, Miriam caught sight of Alan talking to Doctor Nash in the driveway which led to the garage. Apparently Alan spoke rapidly, with quick jerky movements of his hands, while the clergyman contented himself with a nod of his head now and then; suddenly Alan whirled around and went in the direction of the garage. Nash, left to himself, stood still for a minute, then commenced pacing slowly up and down, each turn bringing him nearer the house. Miriam's eyes brightened. Here was her opportunity to deliver Mrs. Nash's message and to talk to Nash undisturbed. Since his arrival in the sick room the night before she had had no chance to speak to him, other than brief statements as to his wife's condition. But she had recognized him instantly upon his entrance as Betty Carter's companion on Monday night.

Leaving the breakfast tray for Martha to take to the pantry, Miriam ran lightly down the staircase and out of the front door. The driveway was entirely clear of snow and at the sound of Miriam's tread on the gravel, Nash looked over his shoulder and halted abruptly.

"Does my wife need me?" he asked. "I'll go to her at once."

"No, wait." Miriam, to her surprise, was breathing rapidly, and paused to recover herself. What was there about this middle-aged man confronting her to make her nervous? A certain hardness about the clean-shaven, handsome mouth, a drooping lid which partly covered one of his blue eyes—no, they did not account for her instinctive dread of the clergyman. She caught Nash's surprise at her continued silence and spoke in haste to cover her embarrassment. "Miss Carter is with your wife."

"Ah, then you are out for a walk. Pardon me for detaining you," and Nash raised his hat, intending to move on, but Miriam checked him.

"Just a moment," she exclaimed. "Your wife wishes you to send for Somers."

"Somers?" questioningly. "Ah, very well. I will go at once and telephone."

"Again I must detain you." Miriam spoke with assurance. She had caught sight of Guy Trenholm as he turned the corner of the house and came toward them. Her eyes brightened. Trenholm had come most opportunely. Unconscious of her added color, she turned to the silent man regarding her, as Trenholm paused by her side.

"Doctor Nash," she began, "I have told Sheriff Trenholm of Miss Carter's visit to Mr. Paul Abbott on Monday night just before he was murdered and that you accompanied her and, in my absence from the sick room, performed the marriage ceremony. Will you kindly confirm that statement?"

Alexander Nash eyed her and Trenholm, then his gaze swept upward to a window of his wife's bedroom where Betty Carter stood looking down at them. His gaze turned again to Miriam and the silent, attentive sheriff.

"On Monday night?" he asked, and his voice was under admirable control. "I fail to recall any such occurrence."

Slowly Miriam took in the meaning of his words. Her face flamed scarlet, then went deadly white.

"You liar! You despicable liar!" she cried, and Trenholm caught her outflung hand. For one moment they confronted each other, then Nash broke the tense pause.

"Hysterics," he commented, pursing up his lips. "Can you manage her, Sheriff, or shall I sent out one of the women?"

Trenholm looked down at Miriam, then across at Nash. "I need no assistance," he said, and the dryness of his voice was not lost on the clergyman. "You need not wait."

Miriam tried to free herself from Trenholm's grasp as Nash went inside the house. Suddenly she ceased struggling and rested limply against him.

"Do you feel better?" he asked, and the human sympathy in his voice almost broke her down. "Shall I get you a glass of wine?"

"No, thanks. I'll be all right in a minute." Miriam straightened up as she regained her self-control. She laid one hand over her rapidly beating heart, but her eyes did not falter in her direct gaze at him. "I owe you an apology for creating a scene."

Trenholm looked at her long and searchingly. From behind a box hedge which skirted the walk, Pierre, the chauffeur, watched the tableau. He was too far away to hear what was said, but the sheriff's expression provided him with food for thought.

Miriam broke the protracted pause. "Doctor Nash does not speak like an American," she said. "What is his nationality?"

Trenholm turned to accompany her into the house. They had reached the veranda before he answered her question.

"Nash is a Canadian," he replied. "Take care—watch that step," as she stumbled.

Miriam slowly released his strong hand, which she had clutched instinctively to keep her balance.

"Thanks!" She looked up again and Trenholm noticed the distended pupils of her eyes. "I shall not trip again."

CHAPTER X
SKIRMISHING

MIRIAM hung up the telephone receiver with a dissatisfied frown. For the third time her talk with the nurse in Doctor Roberts' office had been cut off, and her appeal to the local operator at Upper Marlboro for a clear line had brought no results. Moving away from the telephone table she stood hesitating in the center of the living room. Should she go back to her bedroom and lie down again, or go out for a walk? The latter alternative was the most inviting, although reason told her she should try to sleep. Sleep! She had tossed and turned on her pillow for two mortal hours and never closed her eyes. Always before her was the scene with Alexander Nash and Guy Trenholm. Later, her mind reverted to Betty Carter's denial of her presence at Abbott's Lodge. Twice she had been branded a liar—was she to sit down tamely under it?

Miriam ran softly upstairs to her room, her mind made up. Putting on her coat and hat, she hurried down the hall again, and heard, as she passed Mrs. Nash's partly open bedroom door, the sound of a male voice addressing the sick woman. So Doctor Nash was with his wife! Miriam did not linger.

As she started to close the front door behind her, the telephone bell rang loudly and she hastily entered the living room. Her unexpected return was a trifle disconcerting to Pierre, the chauffeur, who had started from the pantry to answer the telephone. At sight of the nurse standing with the instrument in her hands, he ducked behind the newel post and kept carefully out of sight, while listening intently to what was said.

The call was from the operator at Upper Marlboro, and a second later Miriam was again speaking to Doctor Roberts' office nurse. This time there were no interruptions and Miriam's talk with the nurse was clear and, from her viewpoint, satisfactory. Ten minutes later Miriam was tramping across Abbott's estate, careless as to the direction she was taking, providing it led away from the house of mystery.

Pierre slipped from behind the newel post in time to escape Martha as the latter went about her household work, a reluctant Anna in tow. The murder of Paul Abbott had created a sensation throughout the county, and, as the mystery surrounding the case deepened, the old hunting lodge gained a reputation for ghosts and horrors which kept visitors at a respectful distance, the morbidly curious only daring to venture near it in the daytime. Anna had consented to "help out" provided she did not have to go above the first floor and could be taken home by Corbin in the Abbott car before nine o'clock in the evening. Pierre's attentions, as he waited in the pantry, supplied a new thrill, which the country girl found a pleasant diversion from Martha's sullen irritability and Corbin's unwholesome leers.

It was approaching the luncheon hour when, from his seat by the kitchen window, Pierre perceived Alexander Nash and Corbin talking together on the roadway. Corbin, on his way from the woodshed with a wheelbarrow of wood, had stopped and set down his barrow at a sign from the clergyman. From his gesticulations, Pierre gathered that he was indicating the points of the compass, but the little chauffeur did not wait to see more. Martha's back was turned as she put several pies in the oven, and Anna had gone for an instant into the servants' dining room. Like a flash Pierre was out of the door and up the back staircase to the second floor. His low knock on Mrs. Nash's door was answered by Betty Carter.

"*Bonjour*, Mademoiselle!" he exclaimed, bowing respectfully. "I came to inquire for the health of Madame." His voice carried to Mrs. Nash's sharp ears and she sat up in bed.

"Admit Pierre, Betty," she directed. "I wish to speak to him." At her imperious tone her niece opened the door still further and Pierre stepped inside. With a quick click of his heels, he bowed from the hips, his hands crossed before him, and then advanced.

"Madame is better!" And his respectful tone held a note of genuine relief. Mrs. Nash was a kind mistress and her servants were devoted to her. "Ah, Madame, I have been anxious—yes."

"Thanks, Pierre." Mrs. Nash was touched. She had, with Betty's aid, slipped on a becoming dressing sacque, one of the articles brought from Washington by her husband the evening before, and her boudoir cap was attractively arranged. "Have you heard from Somers?"

"Yes, Madame. Doctor Nash directed her to take the afternoon train for Upper Marlboro, and I will be there to meet her," explained the chauffeur. He turned to Betty. "Your bag, Mademoiselle, came by express just now and Corbin has placed it in your room."

Mrs. Nash understood Betty's quickly checked motion toward the hall.

"Run along, Betty, and see to your bag," she said, good-naturedly. "I don't need you in here every minute, and will ring the bell if I require anything," touching the brass ornament which Martha had resurrected from a china cabinet for her use. "Well, Pierre, have you followed instructions?" she added in a lower key, as Betty vanished out of sight.

Pierre carefully closed the hall door and then came over to the bed, and placed a small paper in Mrs. Nash's outstretched hand. Silently she read the few lines of familiar writing before addressing the expectant servant.

"Where did you find this?" she asked.

Pierre's smile was illuminating. "Corbin has his price," he admitted. "What next, Madame?"

Mrs. Nash sat up a trifle straighter and pointed to the bureau.

"You will find a roll of money in the top drawer," she said. "Bring it over here." Pierre complied with her directions so speedily that she had but a second in which to secrete the paper. Taking the money from the chauffeur, she handed him a generous sum. "Be watchful, Pierre," she cautioned, as he put back the remainder of the bills in their place in the drawer. "Overlook nothing."

"*Oui*, Madame." Pierre halted on his way to the hall door, struck by a sudden idea. "The nurse, Mees Ward—"

"Well, what about her?" as he hesitated.

"She plans to leave to-night."

Mrs. Nash's color changed. "How do you know?" she demanded sharply.

"I heard her telephone to Doctor Roberts to bring another nurse to take her place." Pierre explained, and then waited respectfully for her to address him.

Mrs. Nash viewed the chauffeur in silence and then glanced about the sunny room. It seemed suddenly cold and bare to her. When she spoke her voice had altered to a shriller key.

"As you go along the hall, Pierre, ask my niece to return," she directed, and closing her eyes she laid down again, one hand stroking, as if for companionship, the tongue of the brass bell.

Miriam's walk along the Patuxent River finally brought her to a bridge connecting the highway, and she paused to rest on its parapet. It was a rolling country and she had walked up hill and down dale before striking the river bank. She had put on her high boots for cross-country walking, but she had not found the ground as soft as she anticipated, the snow of four days before having entirely vanished except in a few sheltered nooks and crannies.

The view from the bridge diverted Miriam's thoughts, and she studied the panorama spread before her with interest. Perched high on a hill close at hand was a colonial mansion, its white pillars and gabled roof a fair landmark to be seen for miles, while toward the valley nearer the river, and obviously on the same estate, was a low building, the architecture of which suggested a church or chapel.

Miriam was still speculating on her surroundings when she caught sight of a solitary horseman riding across the fields to her right. The man rode with the unmistakable seat of an American cavalryman, and horse and rider seemed one as they cleared the low fences and swung at last into the highway, headed for the bridge. As he crossed the bridge, Guy Trenholm checked his horse with such suddenness that a shower of mud bespattered Miriam, and his first words, instead of greeting, were an apology.

"Have I ruined your coat?" he asked, in deep contrition, as he sprang to the ground.

"A whisk-broom will remove the damage," Miriam replied lightly. "No, please don't try to rub it off!" as Trenholm drew out his handkerchief. "It must dry first. Where are you going in such a hurry?"

"Not going—returning," he answered. "This is my bailiwick, that—" pointing in the direction from which he had come—"is Anne Arundel County, and my jurisdiction ends at the river's bank."

"And you dignify that stream with the title of river?"

"Don't be so scornful," he protested. "To-day it is a stream, but in the War of 1812 the British men-o'-war sailed up it to this point, burned down the original colonial homestead yonder," indicating the mansion Miriam had been admiring, "and sailed away again."

Miriam was paying scant attention to his historical facts, instead she was considering his previous statement.

"So your jurisdiction ends at the river," she repeated. "And a criminal has simply to run across the bridge to elude you."

"If he is a fast runner," dryly. Trenholm stroked his horse's soft nostril, as the chestnut mare rubbed her head against his arm and nosed in his pocket for the apple and sugar she so dearly loved and always found. "Also, there's a sheriff in Anne Arundel County. Are you returning to Abbott's Lodge, or," his eyes twinkled, "thinking of a sprint across Hills Bridge?"

"My conscience is clear," she replied, "and I am on my way to the Lodge."

"Then let me show you a short cut," and, taking her consent for granted, Trenholm led the way off the high road and along a footpath, his mare walking contentedly along behind them. Miriam, a lover of horses, stopped every now and then to caress her, unconscious of the charming picture she made, her mind carefree for the moment, and her cheeks glowing from her long walk in the wind.

They had gone fully three quarters of the distance to the Lodge when the footpath took a sudden turn to the right and, crossing a wood, skirted a small graveyard. The unexpected sight caused Miriam to start slightly and she took in the air of desolation and the unkept appearance of the graves with a sense of depression which she strove to shake off.

"The Masons' family burying ground," explained Trenholm, observing her change of expression. "It is now part of Abbott's estate. Not a very cheerful sight, is it?"

Miriam shook her head. "Not very," she echoed, and paused idly to count the headstones, some still standing upright, while others, badly chipped and lichen-covered, reclined on the ground. "Twelve," she announced.

"No, thirteen," added Trenholm, pointing to a grave a little distance from the others and running obliquely to them.

"Surely, I didn't see that one," she exclaimed. "Why is it placed in that manner—outside the pale, so to speak?" and she touched a piece of rusty iron which had once formed the fence around the family plot. A number of other upright pieces of iron indicated the line it had once taken.

"It's a suicide's grave," explained Trenholm. "There is an old superstition among the negroes that such a grave cannot be dug straight or on line with the others. Shall we walk on, Miss Ward?" and turning, he whistled to his mare, standing some distance down the path.

They were both rather silent, Miriam, her momentary lapse into her old, gay self, having dropped back into a depression deeper than before, while Trenholm watched her with an absorption of which he was totally unaware.

"I'm afraid you will be late for luncheon," he remarked, happening to glance at his wrist watch as he put his hand on the bridle rein of the mare.

"It doesn't matter," she replied absently. "It won't inconvenience them, for Martha doesn't expect me. I should be asleep, you know."

"You should indeed," he said, and she wondered at his emphatic tone. "This is no preparation for night duty."

"But I am not going on duty to-night," she broke in. "I'm leaving the case."

"What?" Trenholm stopped abruptly and eyed her in concern. "Fired?"

"No, indeed!" She flushed hotly. "Do you suppose I can take care of Mrs. Nash after her husband's treatment of me?"

He did not answer at once. "So you are running away," he commented softly. "Frankly, I did not expect it of you."

"Mr. Trenholm!"

"Running away," he reiterated, paying not the slightest attention to her indignant ejaculation. "Running away under fire."

"Nothing of the sort!" she flared back. "Do you suppose I'll stay in any house where I've twice been called a liar?"

"I'm afraid you'll have to," he retorted, with equal heat. "You cannot leave Abbott's Lodge, Miss Ward."

"What?" She gazed at him astounded. "Why not?"

"Because you are the last person known to have seen Paul Abbott alive," he pointed out slowly. "And your statements regarding the events of Monday night are unsubstantiated."

Miriam stared at him as if unable to believe her ears. "Do you insinuate I lied?" she demanded.

Trenholm's hand on his horse's rein tightened until the knuckles shone white, but his glance did not waver.

"It is not a question of my opinion one way or the other," he said sternly. "You are our chief witness, and as sheriff of Prince Georges County, I cannot permit you to leave Abbott's Lodge."

Miriam regarded him intently. "So that is your attitude," she said, finally. "I am glad to have it defined. You have, at least," with a ghost of a smile, "been honest with me."

"Thank you!" Trenholm drew a step nearer. "Your reasonable acceptance of the situation encourages me to ask a personal question."

"Yes?" she prompted, as he paused. "Well?"

"What is your interest in the black seal?"

Miriam stared at him, thunderstruck. "The black seal?" she repeated.

"Yes—the seal which you have traced many times on paper," and from his coat pocket he drew a number of papers, and held them so that Miriam could see the drawings she had made at odd moments while in the sick room. They were cleverly done—distinct and clear in every detail.

Miriam looked first at them and then up at Trenholm, standing silent and stern by her side.

"Those drawings were in my bag last night," she stammered. "How did you get them?"

"I examined your bag," calmly.

Her eyes were dark with anger. Twice her voice failed her. "You are impossible—intolerable—" she gasped, and turning ran toward Abbott's Lodge, in her blind haste passing Alan Mason without recognition. The latter stopped and stared after her, then catching sight of Guy Trenholm standing patiently by his mare, he whistled softly to himself.

CHAPTER XI
THE FOLDED NOTE

THE undertaker's assistant looked in deep embarrassment at Betty Carter as he remained standing in front of the closed door of the room where lay Paul Abbott's body.

"I'm sorry, Miss," he said. "Those are the sheriff's orders. No one is to go into the room now."

"But why?" demanded Betty. "The funeral will be held in half an hour, and"—her voice quivered—"I want to—to see him before the casket is closed."

Thompson moved uneasily from one foot to the other; Betty's distress disturbed him. "I'm very sorry," he mumbled. "Indeed I am—but it's not possible. Perhaps," his face brightened as the idea occurred to him, "perhaps you can see Mr. Trenholm and get his permission. Here he comes now," as a figure appeared at the far end of the corridor and came toward them. "Oh, pshaw! it's a woman."

Somers, Mrs. Nash's maid, greeted Betty in a subdued voice. "Please, Miss Betty," she said. "Where will I find your aunt? The young woman who let me in declined to come upstairs."

Betty glanced impatiently at the British maid. "Come this way," she turned as she spoke, then hesitated and addressed Thompson. "If you see Sheriff Trenholm tell him, please, I must go in this room."

"Yes, Miss," and Thompson, considerably relieved by the maid's opportune arrival, resumed his slow pacing back and forth before the door.

The sound of his voice and Betty's had carried inside the bedroom, but neither of the two men in it paid the slightest attention. The photographer put up his plates and closed his camera.

"I've taken four views, Mr. Trenholm," he said. "Is that enough?"

Trenholm nodded as he handed the man his flashlight apparatus. "Develop the plates and let me have the prints as quickly as possible," he directed. "Do you need any assistance?" as the photographer shouldered his camera, tripod, and utility box.

"No, thanks." In spite of his haste to be gone, the man was careful to walk as far from the undertaker's couch with its silent figure as the limits of the room permitted. "I'll get these to you to-night. Where shall I send the photographs? Here, or to your home?"

"My home," briefly. Trenholm held open the hall door for him to pass through, then spoke a few whispered words to Thompson. Ten minutes later the body of Paul Abbott had been carried downstairs and the casket closed, while arrangements for the funeral went steadily on.

Trenholm listened impassively to Thompson's flurried delivery of Betty's message, the latter having forgotten it utterly in his astonishment at finding Trenholm had been in the bedroom at the time Betty wished to enter.

"The casket is not to be opened again," the sheriff said sternly. "Understand, Thompson—under no circumstances is it to be opened," and turning he mounted the staircase and found Betty standing at the top landing, waiting for him.

"I heard what you said," she stated. "And would like an explanation of your extraordinary conduct."

"There is nothing extraordinary about it," Trenholm replied quietly. "If you really insist upon an explanation—"

"I do," her passion rising.

"Paul died Monday night—this is Thursday," he spoke gravely. "A change has already set in and it is not possible to keep the casket open longer."

Betty was thankful for the railing of the stairs to lean against.

"I have never been permitted to be with him—"

"I beg your pardon—you have."

"Never alone." She had turned ghastly in color. "Always you have had some one stationed in the room."

Trenholm looked at her in growing concern. "Hadn't you better rest?" he asked. "The funeral will take place in twenty minutes."

Trenholm was doubtful if she heard him, so fixed was her stare. He turned quickly to see what had focused her attention. Standing by the newel post was Alexander Nash in earnest conversation with Alan Mason and a third man, the rector of the Episcopal church at Upper Marlboro. Trenholm laid his hand on Betty's arm. It was shaken off instantly and she shot down the hall to her bedroom without further word. Trenholm stood in thought for several minutes and then joined Alan Mason.

The hands of the grandfather clock in the living room were pointing to three when the funeral services commenced. Betty, accompanied by Alexander Nash, was the last to enter and take the seat reserved for her by Alan Mason's side. A few friends from Washington had motored out to Abbott's Lodge, while the residents in the vicinity had come in a body to attend the services.

Upstairs in her bedroom Mrs. Nash motioned to Somers to come to her, and with reluctance the Englishwoman left her post by the door where she had been keeping an attentive ear for all that was transpiring below.

"Help me up," ordered Mrs. Nash, in a tone Somers had learned not to disregard. "Get my slippers and wrapper." She was panting from her exertions when she finally reached the hall door, a protesting Somers struggling to steady her with a feverish grasp of her elbow.

"Tut, be quiet, Somers; I can't hear a word," and Mrs. Nash appeared in the hall and peered down it. Shifting her husband's cane, which she had picked up on her way from the room, to the other hand, she rested her weight on Somers' arm, and went slowly to the top of the staircase. From there she could hear in the stillness the words of the Episcopal service. When she raised her head after the final prayer, Somers saw that her cheeks were wet with tears.

"I'll rest here," she announced, dropping weakly into a chair by the stairhead. "Oh, it doesn't matter what I'm sitting on," as Somers attempted to remove several overcoats, evidently the overflow from the wraps lying in the living room below. "Bring me the small glass of whisky which Miss Betty poured out before she went downstairs."

In her haste Somers neglected to add any water and Mrs. Nash drank the whisky neat with a wry face. With the false strength engendered by the stimulant, she managed to get back to her room and into bed before her husband came upstairs.

"How are you, dear?" he asked solicitously. "Do you feel stronger?"

"Yes, now that I've taken some whisky," promptly, conscious that the telltale fumes might betray her activities if questioned on the subject. "Are the services over?"

He bowed gravely. "Betty and I are just starting for the cemetery."

"Where is Alan Mason?" sharply.

"He is going with us, also Sheriff Trenholm. Is there anything I can do for you before I leave, Dora?"

"Not a thing, thanks."

Nash looked across the room at Somers; she had her back turned, while engaged in putting Mrs. Nash's lingerie neatly away in the bureau drawer. Stooping over, Nash kissed his wife with unwonted tenderness, then, pressing her hand, hurried away as his name was called by Alan Mason just outside the bedroom door.

A room had been prepared for Somers halfway down the corridor of the right-hand wing of the house, and between Mrs. Nash's periods of dozing the maid succeeded, with Martha Corbin's help, in arranging her belongings to her satisfaction. Somers' methodical mind would not permit her to rest until her own room and that of Mrs. Nash were in apple-pie order. Her trips back and forth took her past Miriam Ward's bedroom and on her final excursion she stumbled over Martha who, not expecting Somers to return so quickly, had knelt down and applied her eye to the keyhole of Miriam's door.

The commotion aroused Miriam from fitful slumber and, springing out of bed, she threw her dressing gown over her shoulders and looked out into the corridor. Somers, rising slowly to her feet, was rubbing a rheumatic knee, while her bewildered eyes followed Martha's fleeing figure.

"Are you hurt?" asked Miriam, noting with surprise the scattered bundle on the floor.

"No, Madam," Somers' precision of speech and her rising intonation clearly denoted her nationality. "A bit shaken," her smile was wintry. "Excuse me for disturbing you."

"Come inside," suggested Miriam kindly, observing that, in spite of her disclaimer, the elderly woman was considerably upset. "Don't stoop over, I will pick up what you dropped. Sit here in this chair," and Somers, after a feeble protest, did as she was told.

"I don't know where that woman sprung from," she added, after describing what had happened. "My arms were full of bed linen and I wasn't looking down. She's a bit uncanny, Miss, don't you think?"

Miriam nodded absently. "Martha is odd," she admitted, as she handed a small dose of aromatic ammonia to Somers. "Drink this and you will feel better."

"Thank you, Miss," exclaimed Somers gratefully, then her mind reverted to Martha. "She wouldn't be so bad, if she wasn't so—so—" casting about for a proper word to express her opinion—"so creepy; and those eyes of hers!" with a shudder. "They give me the horrors."

Miriam smiled, not unkindly. Somers was typical of her class—intelligent, unimaginative, a trifle garrulous and a lover of routine, with a dislike for anything out of the ordinary. And she had come to Abbott's Lodge! Miriam's smile deepened. Judging by her own experiences, the maid was reasonably certain to encounter the unusual if she remained long in attendance on Mrs. Nash.

Somers' honest, comely face grew troubled and she straightened up with a jerk. "I must be getting back to Mrs. Nash," she said. "If you don't mind, Miss, I'll leave the linen here and put it away later in my room."

"How is Mrs. Nash?" asked Miriam, and the maid paused with her hand on the door.

"She was asleep when I left her," responded Somers. "Excuse me, but aren't you Miss Ward?"

"Yes."

"I thought so," and Somers nodded sagely. "Mrs. Nash has told me what you have done for her. She is very fond of you, Miss, and," lowering her voice, "Mrs. Nash can be a very good friend, as well as"—her voice sank to an even lower key—"a good hater."

Miriam eyed the maid in some perplexity. Was her snap-judgment wrong and Somers, instead of a staid, middle-aged Englishwoman, a lover of romance?

Somers gave her no time for reflection. With a murmured word of thanks she went into the hall and closed the door. Miriam walked over to her bureau and consulted her watch—nearly five o'clock. She was in no mood to return to bed. Pulling her dressing gown around her, she prepared a hot bath and, half an hour later, refreshed and invigorated, she stood staring down at her white uniform. Should she put it on, or her house dress? The nurse, sent out from Washington to relieve her, would surely get there in time to go on night duty. If Somers had gotten to Abbott's Lodge so promptly, it would only be a matter of a few hours for the nurse to report for duty. Miriam laid aside her clean uniform and put on her house dress. She had completed her toilet when Martha appeared at the door.

"Please, Miss—Ma'am, Doctor Roberts wishes to see you downstairs," she explained, with characteristic haste. "Say, ain't them lovely?" observing an oddly wrought gold necklace which Miriam slipped inside her gown. "Rubies, ain't they?"

"No, garnets," shortly. Martha's inordinate curiosity was an unpleasant feature. "What were you doing at my door a short time ago?"

Martha's hands twisted in and out of her apron. "I stooped down to pick up a pin and that there clumsy idiot flopped over me," she explained in an aggrieved tone. "Had no better sense than not to look where she was going. She skeered me an'—an'—I ran downstairs." Her tone changed. "Why didn't you come to Mr. Paul's funeral, Miss—Ma'am?" raising her eyes and lowering them rapidly.

Miriam paid not the slightest attention to the question. Stepping past the housekeeper she went in search of Doctor Roberts. He was sitting at the desk in the living room, going over his daybook.

"Good evening, Miss Ward," he exclaimed as she paused in front of him. "I hope Martha did not disturb you. I told her to wait until later."

"I was all ready to come downstairs," she responded. "When will the new nurse be here? Or did she come with you?" glancing hopefully about.

"No." Roberts pocketed his daybook and fountain pen. "After your message came Miss Stockton telephoned to every hospital and the Registry, and not one had a nurse on call."

Miriam stared at him in dismay. "You couldn't get a nurse?" she gasped.

"No, not for to-night, at least; there's an epidemic of grippe and, therefore, a shortage of nurses." Roberts looked at Miriam keenly. "Are you ill, Miss Ward?"

"No; that is"—her bitter disappointment was discernible in her voice. "I can't go on, Doctor."

Roberts rose and walked past the desk, stopping by her side. "What is it, Miss Ward?" he asked sympathetically. "What has happened since this morning?"

She saw his well-cut features, broad brow, and gray hair through a blur. His concern deepened at sight of her evident unhappiness. "What can I do for you?" he asked. "Tell me."

Miriam collected her wits. "I—I'll be myself in a minute," she said, brokenly. "I had hoped to leave the case to-night and was counting on that. I suppose," looking appealingly at him, "that you won't let me off."

"You realize Mrs. Nash's condition as well as I," he replied, and Miriam sighed; she had anticipated such an answer.

"Very well, Doctor. No—" as the scene of the morning rose vividly before her. "I can't nurse that man's wife!"

"What has Nash to do with it?" asked Roberts, in astonishment.

"He denied that he was here on Monday night with Miss Carter," looking straight at Roberts, "and, Doctor, he, a minister of the gospel, lied."

"Well, I'll be—" Roberts checked back the oath with an effort. The silence lengthened as they faced each other. Suddenly the physician turned and paced rapidly up and down, then paused abruptly. "Miss Ward," she looked up at the seriousness of his tone, "you are acquainted with the ethics of our profession. A doctor often becomes cognizant of conditions in a home of which he cannot speak. Alexander Nash's conduct," he paused again, "gives rise to doubt, and, it may be, to investigation. I think," his voice deepened, "that the quicker we get Mrs. Nash on her feet, the sooner will we arrive at a solution of—many things."

Miriam drew in a long breath. "You may be right, Doctor," she admitted. "I'll get into my uniform after dinner."

It was a somber, silent group that drove in the Rolls-Royce from the country cemetery to Guy Trenholm's bungalow five miles distant from Upper Marlboro. Pierre followed the sheriff's directions as to crossroads with indifferent success and Betty finally complained of the rough going and frequent turns.

Trenholm lifted the speaking tube as they approached a white gate which opened on a roadway to a picturesque building partly concealed from the road by a number of trees.

"Stop here, Pierre," he directed, then turned to the silent man by his side. "I am greatly obliged to you, Doctor Nash, for giving me this lift. Good evening," and he sprang out of the car before the chauffeur had brought it to a full stop. Not pausing to exchange a word with Alan or Betty, aside from a wave of his hat, he strode across the turf. As he reached his front door he thrust his hand inside his overcoat pocket for his bunch of keys and pulled them out, and with them a folded piece of paper.

Trenholm stared at the paper as he thrust the key in his front door, and before turning it in the lock, paused to unfold the note. The few lines it bore were unsigned and in an unknown handwriting:

Let him who hopes to solve the mystery of Paul Abbott's death find the lost Paltoff jewel.

Trenholm's expression was as blank as the other side of the paper. It was unaddressed. He reread the note a number of times, then entered his bungalow. The telephone was in the room he used as library and sitting room. Hardly noticing the police dogs that fawned upon him at his entrance, he sat down before the telephone and quickly got his number.

"Hello, constable," he called. "This is Trenholm speaking. Station a guard over the vault where Abbott lies. What's that?—Oh, just a precaution, that's all. Good night!" and he hung up the receiver.

Taking out his pipe and tobacco pouch, he stretched his long legs under the table and sat back, the note in his hand.

"Which one of them," he mused, unaware that he spoke aloud, "slipped this note in my overcoat pocket?"

CHAPTER XII
THE HUMAN EYE

PABLO, Trenholm's Filipino servant, brought the after-dinner coffee into the library and withdrew with the swiftness and silence which characterized his movements.

"Excellent coffee," commented Roberts. He relaxed lazily against the cushioned sides of the big leather chair in which he was sitting and stretched his tired muscles. "It's strong and black. Better have some, Alan."

But Alan Mason declined. "I am too jumpy now," he admitted. "Where the deuce is Trenholm?"

"In the kitchen talking to some man." The physician put down his empty coffee cup and filled it again from the silver pot which Pablo had thoughtfully left on the table, with the sugar and cream. "He'll be back shortly, I imagine; come and sit down," and with his foot he pushed around a chair, similar in size to the one he occupied.

Instead of complying with his invitation, Alan walked moodily about the room, which ran the length of the bungalow. Its ceiling was oak-beamed and the windows diamond-paned, and its air of comfort was enhanced by the good taste evidenced in its furnishing. It was typically a man's room, filled with hunting trophies, smoking paraphernalia, shotgun and rifle, fishing rods and tackle and curious weapons of a bygone age and other climes. Mahogany bookshelves lined one wall and Alan stopped and read the titles of some of the editions.

"Scott, Thackeray, Darwin, Spencer, Dickens, Wells, *et cetera*," he announced, running his finger along the books. "And blame me, if they don't look as if he'd read 'em."

Roberts turned his head to observe what Alan was doing. "Trenholm is one of the best informed men in the country," he remarked dryly. "He is well read and has a brilliant mind."

"And lives in this God-forsaken part of the country!" Alan shrugged his shoulders. "There is no accounting for taste."

"Quite so!" Roberts laughed. "But if my memory serves me right, Alan, you are indigenous to the soil."

"Sure, but my parents had the good sense to move to Washington soon after I was born," retorted Alan. "We spent only our summers here until Cousin Paul Abbott bought the old place in a land deal."

"Oh, so Abbott's Lodge is your ancestral homestead?"

Alan nodded. "With many alterations and additions," he said. "I'd never have known the house when I first went to stay with Paul just before the War. We were at Lawrenceville together, you know, and then at Princeton." Alan sighed. "The War changed him a lot," he added wistfully. "He was a dandy pal—so much pep and devil-may-care spirit about him."

"When was he shell-shocked?"

"Toward the last." Alan changed the subject with marked abruptness. "Say, Doctor," he sat down and his voice dropped to a confidential pitch. "Trenholm does himself mighty well—this most attractive bungalow, a model farm, and a servant whose cooking is absolutely faultless. Where does he get the money?"

"His salary—"

Alan laughed mirthlessly. "It wouldn't much more than pay Pablo's wages," he said. "It takes real money to keep up a place like this."

Roberts lighted a cigar, first offering one to Alan, which the latter accepted, with a word of thanks.

"I heard some time ago that a rich relation—one of the Trenholms of South Carolina—died and left Guy a handsome legacy, which he has augmented by careful investments," he explained.

"Oh!" Alan was having some difficulty in lighting his cigar. "Who told you that—Trenholm?"

"I believe so. Why?" His question met with no response and Roberts eyed his companion in speculative silence.

Alan's complexion was not a healthy color, the physician decided in his own mind, and the unsteadiness of his hand as he strove to hold a match to his cigar was not lost on Roberts. The older man's expression grew thoughtful; Alan Mason had changed in the past few days and not for the best. Roberts had observed his tendency to go off alone for long walks, and his sudden bursts of talkativeness at the table and his equally abrupt lapses into long, sullen silence from which no one could arouse him.

It was in such a fit of depression that Roberts had encountered him when about to motor over to Trenholm's for dinner, and he had persuaded Alan to accompany him after the latter had first called up Trenholm and received a hearty invitation to make one of the party. All through dinner Alan had chatted on first one topic and then another, the others seconding his efforts, but the three men with one accord avoided any reference to the tragedy at Abbott's Lodge or to the funeral which had taken place that afternoon.

Trenholm found his two guests smoking in silence when he joined them a few minutes later.

"Sorry to have been so long," he said apologetically, taking up a cup of coffee, before seating himself on the divan before the open fire. "There have been a number of petty thefts in the neighborhood, but I believe we've jailed the right man to-day, from the evidence just brought to me." He swallowed his coffee and replaced the cup on the table. "By the way, Roberts, how is Mrs. Nash?"

"Much better this evening," responded Roberts. "If she continues to show such improvement, she may be able to sit up to-morrow for a time."

"Ah, then Mrs. Nash can soon dispense with the services of a trained nurse," broke in Alan, with a swift look upward at the clock on the mantel.

"Perhaps," answered Roberts. "Much depends, however, on what sort of a night she has."

"Is Miss Ward still on the case?" questioned Trenholm, knocking the ashes from his pipe before refilling it.

"Yes." Roberts puffed silently at his cigar for a few seconds. "I tried to get another nurse to relieve her, but none were disengaged."

"So Miss Ward told you she wished to go?" with a quiet persistence which made Roberts glance at the sheriff in surprise.

"Yes. Why?"

"I wondered if she would attempt to leave after all," responded Trenholm. "I warned her that she was wanted here until after the inquest."

"Wanted?" Alan dropped the cigar from his nervous fingers and hastily stooped to pick it up. When he sat back his face was flushed. "Wanted—for what?"

"As chief witness. Hello, who's here?"—as the knocker on the front door sounded in three hurried blows.

Pablo, busy in clearing off the dining room table, scurried into the hall and the murmur of voices sounded first faintly and then came distinctly to their ears. The three men gazed blankly at each other as Pablo pulled back the portières.

"Mees Carter," he announced and discreetly vanished.

"Betty!" Alan was the first on his feet. "Why are you here?"

Betty's glance swept by him to Roberts and then to her host.

"I wish to see you, Guy Trenholm," she said. "Why have you put a guard around the vault where Paul lies?"

As she came further into the library, the men saw that the hem of her short walking suit and her high boots were splashed with mud. Trenholm pulled back a chair and stepped toward her.

"So that his grave will not be molested," he replied quietly. "There are ghouls who, attracted by the newspaper accounts of Paul's tragic death, would not hesitate to enter the vault if given an opportunity. You have been there to-night?"

"That is obvious," with a glance at her muddy condition and the smart walking stick which she carried. Her hair, naturally curly, showed under the brim of her sport hat, and her cheeks were rosy from the cold night air. But to Trenholm's keen vision, there was a strained look about her eyes, a continuous twitching of her hands which betrayed nerves keyed to the highest tension. "Doctor Roberts," she turned impulsively to the older man, ignoring Alan, "has Sheriff Trenholm told you his theory of the murder?"

Roberts looked from her to Trenholm. "No," he replied, and would have added more, but Trenholm cut in.

"I have not discussed my theories with any one," he said smoothly. "But your suggestion is a good one. Sit here," dragging forward a chair, "and we will talk the situation over. Doctor Roberts, you and Alan—and perhaps"—his smile was enigmatic. He did not complete his sentence, but waited patiently for Betty to seat herself.

With a swift glance about her she mastered her hesitation—her inclination to run away. She had come there with a purpose, and until that was accomplished—her fingers clenched about her stick; it required all her self-control not to strike the tall man at her elbow. He dwarfed her in size, but the smoldering resentment in her eyes flamed up as he bent toward her.

"Do sit down," repeated Trenholm with gentle insistence. "Take your old chair, Roberts," and he dropped into one next the physician as Alan and Betty followed his example. "Now, Miss Carter—" he prompted.

Betty glanced at him for a fraction of a second, then her gaze swept the library. It was the first time she had ever been in Trenholm's house. Slowly her eyes traveled about the room, noting each object, until finally her gaze rested on a large silver frame standing on the big mahogany table. It was one she had given to Trenholm in Paris. She caught her breath slightly—the frame was empty. She suddenly grew conscious of the concentrated regard of her companions and involuntarily her glance sought Alan, sitting across from her.

"Well, Betty, we are waiting," he exclaimed.

"For the sheriff," she broke in. "Come, sir, do not keep us longer."

Trenholm took out a cigarette case and offered it to Betty, but she waved it away. "I'll take some coffee," she said. "Thanks, Alan," as he filled a cup for her. Again she turned to Trenholm. "Go on."

"Suppose we reconstruct the scene on Monday night," began Trenholm slowly. "Roberts turns Paul over to his trained nurse and leaves. Corbin and his wife go to bed, and Miss Ward is alone with her patient...."

"What then?" asked Alan, bending forward, his eyes fastened on Betty, who sat sipping her coffee. Trenholm answered his question with another.

"What do we know of Miss Ward?" he asked, and Roberts stared at him.

"Know of her?" the physician repeated. "She was sent on the case by Central Registry."

"And what about her antecedents?" questioned Trenholm. "Where did she spring from? Is she a Washingtonian?"

"She said not," replied Roberts. "She told me that she had trained in New York."

"And you know nothing more of her than that?"

"Nothing more."

"You don't even know that she was not acquainted with Paul before."

"What!" Roberts' eyes opened as well as his mouth. "Why—why—they were strangers."

"Ah, were they?" with quiet emphasis. "Can you prove it?"

Roberts shook his head. "No; but judging from her manner she had never met Paul before."

"Women are clever actresses," retorted Trenholm. "Well, Miss Ward, who may or who may not have known Paul before, is the last person known to have been with him on the night he was murdered—the last person to have seen him alive!"

"Hold on," the interruption came from Alan. He was not looking at Betty, but kept his eyes steadfastly lowered, the cigar still in his hand. "Miss Ward claims that Paul had visitors—"

"And Miss Ward's statements as to their presence have not been substantiated"—Trenholm paused and Betty could not avoid his stare—"as yet."

In the lengthening silence Betty's rapid breathing was faintly audible. She finished her coffee and her hand was quite steady as she set the cup and saucer down on a stool by her side.

"And your theory is—what?" she asked, raising her eyes to Trenholm's.

"That Miss Ward killed Paul while he slept," replied the sheriff.

Alan drew out his handkerchief and wiped his forehead. "It's a rotten theory!" he exploded. "Why, Trenholm, I thought you liked Miss Ward?"

Betty shot a swift glance at Trenholm and her figure grew rigid.

"It is not a matter of like or dislike," replied Trenholm quietly. "It's a question of finding Paul's murderer. You asked me for a theory—and mine is a reasonable hypothesis."

"Just a moment," broke in Roberts. "Paul was no slight weight. I doubt if Miss Ward could have lifted him in and out of bed unassisted, especially putting him back in bed—a dead body is an unwieldy object."

"She could have killed him in bed," replied Trenholm.

"But the other night you pointed out to Miss Ward and me that the lack of bloodstains on the sheets proved the crime was not committed in the bed," objected Alan heatedly.

Trenholm eyed him thoughtfully. "You forget Miss Ward is a nurse," he pointed out slowly. "It would be a simple matter for her to change the bed linen with the dead man lying in it."

Betty leaned forward in her earnestness. "And what became of the bloodstained sheets?" she asked.

Trenholm uncrossed his long legs and leaned closer to her chair. "Ask Corbin," he suggested.

Betty's grasp of her walking stick tightened, and she grew conscious of the atmosphere of the overheated room. Turning from Trenholm's direct gaze she saw Alan fumbling with his collar, his face a pasty white, and she seized her opportunity to divert attention from herself.

"Are you ill, Alan?" she asked, her eyes big with concern. "Doctor, can't we have some fresh air in the room?"

Roberts threw up the window nearest to him, then went to Alan's aid. Alan took the flask Trenholm proffered and drank eagerly, putting it down almost empty.

"I'm better," he announced. "The room's infernally hot. Say, Guy," turning impulsively to him, "your theory's no good. What possible motive could Miss Ward have had to kill Paul?"

"Frankly, I don't know"—there was something disarming about Trenholm's smile and Alan's anger cooled. "Miss Carter asked for a theory and I gave her one."

Betty shrugged her shoulders. "Which won't hold water." Her voice altered and her companions gathered a hint of pent-up passion as she added, in tones which she strove to steady, "Paul's murder was no motiveless crime."

"Quite so," agreed Trenholm. "And that motive was what, Miss Carter?" He waited in vain for an answer, and finally broke the pause. "Paul apparently had no enemies, and yet he was killed," he said. "Come, Roberts, you've known and loved the boy for years; you, Alan, were his first cousin and chum; Miss Carter, his," he paused, and she looked at him dumbly, "his one love. Among you, can you not tell the motive which inspired Paul's murder—was it hate, was it revenge, was it greed?"

His deep voice lingered on the last word, then ceased. Roberts had touched him on the arm. At a sign from the physician Trenholm, without moving, turned his head and glanced at the open window. The light from one of the lamps shone directly on the outer blind. It had been turned a crack and in it peered a human eye.

With a spring which carried him halfway across the room, Trenholm gained the hall and threw open the front door, his police dogs at his heels. They swept by him and raced around the house and down the driveway, the sheriff and Roberts behind them. As the dogs gave tongue, a strong, powerful voice called Trenholm's name.

"Call off your dogs, Trenholm!" And turning his flashlight on the newcomer, the sheriff recognized Alexander Nash, the Rolls-Royce standing down the roadside.

In the library Betty turned aside from her feverish scanning of Trenholm's papers on the table, to find Alan standing, with his back partly turned, drinking the remaining whisky out of the flask. Betty was by his side in an instant.

"Stop, Alan; you mustn't!" she pleaded, real terror in her handsome eyes. "You promised me—"

Alexander Nash's heavy tread, as he and Roberts entered the room, caused her to swing swiftly in their direction.

"Your aunt was alarmed by your absence, Betty," explained Nash, and his voice sounded loudly in the sudden stillness. "She learned of your trip to the cemetery and sent me to bring you home."

CHAPTER XIII
THE SPIDER AND THE FLY

MIRIAM WARD opened the window a little further and looked out. It was nearly midnight and the cold, raw breeze was an agreeable contrast to the atmosphere of the sick room. Mrs. Nash's preparations for the night were long-drawn-out and Miriam had found her at her worst. In turn she waxed dictatorial, fault-finding and fretful, and Miriam's stock of patience was severely taxed. It seemed an interminable time before Mrs. Nash finally closed her eyes with the avowed intention of taking "forty winks," and the imperative command that she be awakened the moment her husband returned.

Miriam made herself as comfortable as possible on the window seat, having carried a sofa pillow with her, and pulling her sweater more closely over her shoulders, she leaned her head against the wooden sash and stared out into the night. The stars were out and the moonlight added beauty to the grounds. It all appeared so calm and peaceful, so utterly different from the last four hectic days. Miriam sighed involuntarily and closed her eyes. When she opened them a few minutes later she saw the powerful headlights of a car coming along the turnpike. A second later it had swung into the driveway and Miriam recognized the Rolls-Royce. The front door was toward the other side of the house, and Miriam lost sight of the car as it circled the approach to the *porte cochère*. Undoubtedly Doctor Nash had returned.

Miriam's expression hardened. Her outspoken, frank disposition made it next to impossible for her to cloak her aversion even under the ordinary courtesies of the sick room. She was commencing to loathe Doctor Nash; while wondering dimly why two such opposite natures as Dora Carter and the clergyman had ever fallen in love with each other. Truly, the marriage market was but a lottery!

Leaving her position by the window, Miriam walked softly over to the bed. Her patient's deep breathing assured her that Mrs. Nash was comfortably asleep and Miriam's heart lightened; she would not have to summon Doctor Nash, for, in spite of his wife's wishes, Miriam did not propose to awaken her. The closing of a door further down the hall with a resounding bang brought her hand to her heart and Mrs. Nash's eyes unclosed in time to notice Miriam's agitation.

"What was that noise?" she demanded. "What has happened to make you so pale?"

"Nothing—it's the lamplight," Miriam stammered a trifle incoherently. "A door slammed and startled me."

Mrs. Nash rubbed her eyes and inspected her with interest. Miriam's trig uniform was becoming.

"Nerves," Mrs. Nash remarked caustically. "Have you seen Doctor Nash?"

"He has just returned and I believe is still downstairs," responded Miriam. "But, Mrs. Nash, you should not see any one at this hour."

"Tut! My nap has refreshed me, and besides, I am stronger, much stronger," with emphasis, and she struggled into a sitting position. "Just throw that bed sacque over my shoulders and ask Doctor Nash to come here, there's a good child!"

Miriam's hesitation was interrupted by a low tap on the bedroom door, and walking swiftly over to it she found Doctor Roberts standing in the hall.

"I am on my way to bed," he said, softly. "How is Mrs. Nash?"

"Her general condition is better now." Miriam slipped outside and held the door so that their voices would not carry into the bedroom. "But when I came on duty I found her cyanosed, so I gave her stimulation and applied heat locally."

Doctor Roberts stroked his chin thoughtfully, then moved toward the door and Miriam held it open. Mrs. Nash greeted him with a frown.

"Some more horrid medicine," she grumbled. "Well, all paths lead to the grave."

"A cheerful outlook," smiled Roberts as he took her pulse. "You ought to be asleep at this hour."

"I never felt more wakeful," and Mrs. Nash's alert look confirmed her words. "Where have you been all the evening?"

"At Sheriff Trenholm's—Alan Mason and I dined with Trenholm, and your husband drove us back."

"What was he doing there?" The look which she flashed at him startled the physician.

"He had come for Betty Carter, having missed her at the cemetery," replied Roberts. He was commencing to feel uncomfortable under Mrs. Nash's steady stare. Quickly he rose to forestall other questions. "We returned together a few minutes ago. Now, Mrs. Nash, it is after midnight and you must get to sleep."

"Presently," she retorted. "As you go to your room, Doctor, please ask Alex to come here. I shall not sleep until I have seen my husband," and her air of finality closed the discussion. "Good night."

Roberts smiled at her characteristic dismissal. At the door he turned to Miriam and signed to her to come into the hall.

"Humor her as much as possible," he said. "When she gets her own way, she'll go to sleep. Her pulse is better and she has no temperature. I'll send Nash along," and with a friendly smile he hurried downstairs.

Miriam had just given Mrs. Nash a drink of water when the clergyman came in. Mrs. Nash's sharp, black eyes detected his constrained manner as he spoke to Miriam and her equally stiff acknowledgment of his greeting. Turning her back upon Nash, Miriam addressed his wife.

"I will wait in the alcove in the hall until your husband leaves," she said. "If you wish anything, please let me know."

Nash remained standing until the hall door closed behind Miriam and then he seated himself in a chair by his wife's bed.

"I am so thankful that you are better, Dora," he said, taking her hand in both his and raising it to his lips. "So very, very thankful to a merciful Providence."

"Save some of your thanks for Miss Ward," she remarked dryly. "She gave Providence a helping hand. By the way, you don't seem to like her."

"My dear Dora!"

"Why not?" she persisted, ignoring his interjection.

Nash sighed. Custom had taught him respect for his wife's tenacity, but there were times when he wanted to shake her.

"She, eh—reh—has an agreeable personality," he began. "I am grateful to her for what she has done for you, but I, eh, really, my dear, haven't given her much thought."

"Oh!" Nash squirmed uneasily under her unswerving gaze. "Oh!" repeated Mrs. Nash, and her intonation conveyed much or little according to her husband's perception. "And Betty, where is she?"

The rapid change of topic confused Nash, his slower wits failing to keep up with his wife's trend of thought. "She is downstairs," he stated. "That is, I left her there talking to Alan and Roberts."

"She ought to be in bed," declared Mrs. Nash, with ill-concealed irritability. "Traipsing around the countryside by herself at night. Did she reach the cemetery?"

"Yes." Nash cleared his throat. "The attendant at the vault told me that she had gone to Trenholm's, two miles the other side of the cemetery; so Pierre drove me there and I brought her home."

Mrs. Nash looked down at the old-fashioned, handmade quilt and studied its pattern and cross stitch intently.

"Betty is a great responsibility," she said, glancing over at her husband. "Her eccentric conduct, her total lack of thought for others—"

"She is young," broke in Nash with some vehemence and his wife changed color. "And youth is selfish."

"If that were all—" Mrs. Nash spoke under her breath and her husband failed to catch what she said. He did not care to break the pause and, as the silence lengthened, Mrs. Nash's thoughts reverted to the past.

Alexander Nash did not appear a day older than the first time she had met him in London two years before. The fact that he was again clean-shaven accounted for his unaltered appearance, his wife decided. She had never cared for his carefully trimmed beard and mustache which he had worn until a day or so before. A flood of memories of the days of their courtship, their marriage in Paris and their happy, happy honeymoon kept Mrs. Nash silent. A year and six months had passed since then. Mrs. Nash bit her lip.

"I am a romantic old fool," she admitted, and her usually metallic tones had softened, holding a depth of feeling which would have startled her skeptic friends. "Kiss me, Alec."

From where she sat in the hall Miriam caught now and then the sound of voices from the living room on the floor below, and recognized Betty's clear tones and Roberts' heavier bass, with now and then a word from Alan Mason. But from Mrs. Nash's bedroom no sound issued and she waited patiently in her corner for Doctor Nash to take his departure. Footsteps on the staircase caused her to draw further back in the alcove; she was in no mood to talk to any member of the house party that night. Was "house party" the proper term when tragedy had brought them together under the same roof? With a shake of her head Miriam dismissed the question as Betty came up the steps, followed by Roberts. On reaching the second floor she paused and spoke to the physician.

"I cannot sleep," Miriam heard her say. "Indeed, Doctor, I cannot sleep, and another night like the last three will drive me to madness. Can't you give me something to induce sleep?"

Roberts scanned her closely. Betty's broken voice, her quivering lips which she strove vainly to keep steady, were both unmistakable symptoms of her overwrought condition. Roberts had marveled at her self-control during their drive homeward, unexpectedly delayed by a puncture which had taken Pierre over an hour to repair. Nash's wrath at the chauffeur for not having a spare tire along had added a picturesque moment to the monotony of the trip. It was the first time Roberts had seen the generally self-contained clergyman give way to temper.

"Get ready for bed, Betty," Roberts advised, "and I will ask Miss Ward to prepare a sedative."

Betty checked him with an expressive gesture. "Can't you give it to me?" she asked. "I—I dislike to—to ask Miss Ward for—for—to do anything," she spoke through chattering teeth. "I believe I am having a chill."

Roberts laid a firm hand on her arm. "Come," he said in tones which his patients rarely disobeyed. "Go immediately to bed. I will find Miss Ward to assist you; now, no nonsense," as she paused to voice another objection. "Go."

Miriam emerged from the alcove as Roberts, after conducting Betty to her bedroom door, came down the hall.

"Doctor Nash is with his wife," she explained. "I have been sitting yonder and could not help but overhear your conversation with Miss Carter."

"She is on the point of a breakdown," Roberts said tersely. "Is your hypodermic ready for use?"

"Yes, Doctor."

"Then please come to Miss Carter's bedroom: I will meet you there in a few minutes," and taking her acquiescence for granted Roberts hurried to his own room where he had left his bag.

Miriam paused in indecision; she had been trained to serve humanity—to care for the sick and to look after the infirm. Was it obligatory upon her to minister to Betty now that she was ill? No, a thousand times, no! From somewhere came the chimes of a clock—one in the morning—Doctor Roberts was powerless to secure other aid in a sick room at that hour and twenty miles from Washington. Miriam walked quietly to her room, where she had her hypodermic syringe, secured it and went direct to Betty. Alexander Nash would find her if she was needed by his wife.

Betty looked up at her approach and Miriam was struck by the suffering in her face. In her haste to undress and get into bed she had scattered her clothes on the floor and she had kept on her dressing gown.

"It—it's very good of you," she murmured. "I—I—" she paused, at a loss for words.

"Doctor Roberts will be here in a moment," answered Miriam quietly. Putting down her hypodermic, she spent the next few minutes arranging the room and adjusting the windows. Betty never took her eyes from her and Miriam was thankful when Roberts knocked on the closed door.

Silently Miriam aided him in his examination and her swift deftness won his admiration. As he took the thermometer from Betty Miriam observed a gold chain suspended about her neck. She caught Miriam's glance and drew her dressing gown close about her throat.

Miriam prepared the hypodermic, then paused by Roberts' side. "Will you give it?" she said simply, holding the instrument toward the physician, and Roberts grasped her reluctance to administer the opiate.

No one in the room was aware that the door had been cautiously opened an inch or two and then as quietly closed. Alan Mason reached the staircase a minute later and stood listening, his head bent. Only the faint tick-tock of the grandfather clock was to be heard. Convinced that he was alone in the hall he made his way noiselessly to the door of the room where Paul Abbott's body had lain until the funeral that afternoon. The door was locked. Alan drew in his breath sharply, hitched at his dark sweater, and glanced down at his "sneakers"; then he crept softly through the darkness of the back hall and disappeared.

Roberts looked over at Miriam and then at Betty as he rose and tiptoed to the door. "She will be all right, now," he said. "If you have an opportunity, come in again during the night." He paused and, to Miriam's surprise, held out his hand. "Thank you. Good night."

Miriam delayed only a few seconds to adjust the light so that it would not shine directly in Betty's eyes and awaken her, and then she left the room. She had almost reached her old seat in the alcove, and was debating in her mind whether or not to go at once into Mrs. Nash's room, when her patient's door swung open and Doctor Nash appeared in the hall. He looked relieved to find her there.

"I waited until my wife dropped asleep," he said. "You can go in now, but pray don't disturb her."

Miriam bit her lip to keep back a heated rejoinder. Instructions in nursing from members of the patient's family, irrespective as to who they were, were generally infuriating, but, from Alexander Nash, doubly so. He evidently expected no answer, for turning abruptly, he sought his bedroom.

Nash had not only lowered the lamp before leaving his wife, but had placed a screen about it—however Miriam's familiarity with the room enabled her to move about without colliding with the furniture. The cot did not appeal to her—she felt, as she had once expressed it to a fellow student at the hospital when in training, too "twitchy" to lie down. Going over to the chair which Nash had occupied, she sat down in it. It was not the one which customarily stood near the bed, but another chair, bigger and much lower, and Miriam experienced a sense of sudden shock as she dropped down further than she had expected.

It was a chair built for a large man and Miriam felt lost in its depths and squirmed back, hoping to find an easier position, but that made her stretch her legs before her at an uncomfortable angle. Too tired to get up, she put her hand behind her and pulled up the seat cushion. As she did so, she touched a paper—evidently a letter, she judged, as she ran her fingers over what was unmistakably an envelope with stamps upon it. Half rising she turned around and bending down saw that a letter was wedged between the high, tufted cushion and the upholstered back of the chair. In idle curiosity, Miriam took it up, replaced the cushion, and carried the letter over to the lamp. The orange Canadian stamps caught her attention instantly. She turned it over. The black seal was unbroken, the flap uncut—the letter evidently never had been opened.

Miriam drew a long, long breath. Turning, she gazed at the chair. Its unwieldy size had induced her to push it behind the bedroom door the first night of Mrs. Nash's illness, to get it out of the way. Evidently Doctor Nash had preferred it to the one in which she generally sat, and had moved it up to the bed. Had he accidentally dropped the letter in the chair and not perceived it when leaving the darkened room? Miriam consulted the postmark and then the address. It bore Paul Abbott's name and was dated January 23, 1923.

Miriam stood in deep thought holding the unopened letter, then she slipped it inside her uniform, made sure that it was safe, and, crossing the room, seated herself once more by Mrs. Nash, her mind in a turmoil.

It was close upon three o'clock in the morning when Mrs. Nash awoke and called Miriam by name.

"I am so thirsty," she complained, as the girl bent over her. "Couldn't I have some orange juice?"

"Certainly," and Miriam went over to the table on which she kept her supplies. The oranges were there, but hunt as she might, she could find no knife. With a few uncomplimentary comments on Martha's carelessness in neglecting to bring her one when she carried her night lunch upstairs, Miriam hastened down to the pantry, after a brief word of explanation to Mrs. Nash.

Mrs. Nash could see from her position in the bed the hall door which Miriam had left ajar; from there her gaze shifted to the lighted lamp at the farther end of the room, and then she closed her eyes. When she opened them the bedroom was in darkness.

As Mrs. Nash lay speechless with surprise, she grew conscious that some one beside herself was in the room, and a faint, scraping noise sounded closer and closer to the bed. Suddenly something soft brushed across the back of her hand lying on the edge of her bed. Turning her hand over with lightning speed, her fingers closed spasmodically upon some object, and a cry escaped her.

Miriam, halfway up the stairs, covered the distance to her bedroom with flying feet as the low cry came to her ears. She faltered in consternation at sight of the utter darkness. Mrs. Nash caught sight of her white uniform as she stood in the doorway, outlined by the light behind her in the hall.

"Bring in the lamp," she directed, unaware that her voice was hoarse from excitement, and Miriam obeyed her instantly. When she reached the bedside, Mrs. Nash was leaning upon her elbow, a false beard suspended from her hand.

"I almost got him," she exclaimed in triumph, then fainted quietly away.

———————————————————

CHAPTER XIV
THE WILL OF HATE

DOCTOR ROBERTS leaned back in his chair and stared at Guy Trenholm.

"So, Paul, poor lad, was stabbed with that vicious-looking nut pick," he exclaimed, pointing to where it lay on the table in the sunparlor of Abbott's Lodge. "And Mrs. Nash was awakened last night by a disguised man and succeeded in dragging off his false beard. Upon my word—what next?"

The two men, with Alan Mason, looking wretchedly ill, making a poor third in their conversation, were waiting patiently for the arrival from Washington of the lawyer employed by Paul Abbott, who had signified his intention of reaching there at ten o'clock. It was then eleven, as Alan's frequent glances at his watch assured him, and his nervousness was increasing. He looked up furtively at Roberts at the latter's question.

"Did Mrs. Nash recognize the man?" he asked.

Roberts shook his head. "She said she was unable to make out if it was a man or a woman—"

"A woman!" Alan dropped the penknife with which he was fiddling and half rose. "*A woman?* Why, that's a man's beard in your hand, Guy."

"But a woman could have disguised herself with it, as well as a man," Trenholm said. "Odd, isn't it, that something always happens to Miss Ward's patients when she is on duty."

"For God's sake, why are you forever picking on her!" Alan dropped back in his chair and his voice rang out indignantly, reaching the ears of Betty Carter, who was eating a belated breakfast in the dining room.

Betty's violent start was not lost on Martha, and the housekeeper decided to remain in the room under pretext of rearranging the silver in the drawer. But first she handed a plate of toast to Betty and as the girl took a slice she encountered the unfriendly stare of Martha's oddly assorted eyes and an involuntary shiver ran down her spine. Her attention distracted, Betty failed to distinguish any reply to Alan's fervid question and, not having heard Trenholm's remark which had called it forth, she was in doubt to whom the "her" referred. Who was Guy Trenholm "picking on" now? She longed to steal to the closed portières and overhear what was being said, but Martha's presence kept her in her seat.

The opiate had given her needed sleep and Betty felt more like her old self once again. Against the advice of Somers, Mrs. Nash's maid, who had gone early to inquire how she was, she had insisted upon getting up and coming downstairs. Somers had regaled her, while in the process of assisting her to dress, with a dramatic account of Mrs. Nash's adventures that night—and they lost nothing in the telling. Betty's rapt attention would have inspired an even less imaginative person to thrilling heights of fancy. A burst of tears relieved the tension of Betty's overtaxed nervous system and reduced Somers to contrite silence. Had not Doctor Roberts as well as Miss Ward cautioned her not to excite Miss Betty? Somers' confused state of mind was not lessened by Betty's reception of a piece of news which the maid let drop incautiously—the expected arrival of Daniel Corcoran, for many years attorney and close friend of the elder Abbott and the legal adviser of the latter's son. Betty's feverish desire to dress and have her breakfast downstairs took away Somers' breath and she retired thankfully, a short time later, to the comparative tranquillity of Mrs. Nash's bedroom.

Unaware of Betty's presence in the dining room Roberts and Trenholm continued their low-voiced conversation.

"Have you made tests for fingerprints on the nut pick, Trenholm?" inquired Roberts.

The sheriff nodded. "An expert came down from Washington," he answered. "Aside from the bloodstains, there were no marks upon it. Evidently the person using it"—Trenholm held up the nut pick in its wrapping of oil silk as he spoke and then placed it carefully in the inside pocket of his coat— "wore gloves. As a means of identification the bit of steel is a failure."

"An ingenious weapon," commented Roberts. "And Paul's pyjamas' jacket offered no resistance. It would not have required great strength to drive the pick into a vital part of his body—"

"There you go again," objected Alan, "insinuating the murder was committed by a woman. Say, you are a great sheriff, you are!" turning in sudden, unlooked-for wrath to the big man lounging near him. "Why don't you do something besides loaf around this place? I believe you were here last night!"

"Was I?" Trenholm's calm smile was provoking in its hint of bored amusement. Was the sheriff poking fun at him? The thought was intolerable, and Alan jerked uneasily about and finally rose and strolled over to one of the glass doors leading to the garden. "Well, this appears to be the place a sheriff is needed, Alan. First the cold-blooded murder of a defenseless man," his voice rose slightly—"then a housebreaker last night—"

"Deuce take it!" Roberts straightened up and laid down his cigar. "Something must be done, Trenholm; Alan's right. Why not try one of the well-known detective agencies?"

"Perhaps I may, shortly," Trenholm rejoined in the same unemotional tones. "I am always open to suggestions. Have you any more, Alan?"

Alan's white cheeks turned a more healthy color and leaving the window he came closer to Trenholm; stopped, opened his mouth to speak, hesitated, then moved over to the portières. Parting them slightly he gazed into the dining room. It was vacant.

"Listen, Guy;" he had regained Trenholm's side and spoke hurriedly, clipping his words together. "What about Corbin? Have you thought of him as a— a—possible suspect?"

Trenholm stared up at his agitated questioner for a moment in silence. "Corbin tells an apparently straight tale, Alan," he replied. "He declares that after admitting Miss Ward on Monday evening he and Martha retired to their rooms and slept soundly all night. Their quarters, as you know, are near the roof and at the back of the house. No ordinary sound would carry that distance."

"What do you mean by an ordinary sound?" asked Roberts, who was following the rapid dialogue with deep attention.

"A door bell, for instance," responded Trenholm, with a quick glance at Alan.

Alan looked away for an instant. "How about a sound *out* of the ordinary?" he demanded. "A cry of terror—of horror—wouldn't that reach them?"

Trenholm shook his head dubiously. "Not with their doors closed. And Martha substantiates her husband's statement that they are both heavy sleepers."

"Oh, Martha!" Alan tossed down his hat which he had picked up and held aimlessly, twirling it back and forth. "I wouldn't believe her on oath—neither of them, for that matter. Why under heaven Paul kept the Corbins here after his father's death I cannot imagine."

"Possibly because he deemed them faithful," replied Trenholm dryly. "You must also recollect that it is difficult to induce servants to live out here in the country all the year round."

Alan, silenced but not convinced, walked sulkily across the sunparlor and threw himself into a wicker chair. "The Washington papers are still featuring the murder," he said, pointing to a newspaper lying on the floor with a headline running half across the front page. "I'm tired of heading off the reporters."

"Send them to me," suggested Trenholm.

"You!" disgust spoke in Alan's voice. "They call you the fresh water clam of Prince Georges County. You've got their goat by your uncommunicative ways and rotten bad manners."

Trenholm looked across at Roberts. "I don't appear to be popular," he remarked, a faint twinkle in his eye, and changed the subject. "Will you throw me that false beard, Doctor?"

Roberts handed it to him. "Any clue in that, Trenholm?" he asked, watching the sheriff stow it carefully away in his coat pocket.

"Maybe. I've only had it in my possession for the past hour." The wicker chair in which Trenholm was seated creaked under his weight as he straightened up from his lounging position, preparatory to rising. "When can I interview Mrs. Nash, Doctor?"

"This afternoon, I imagine," answered Roberts. "I saw her before breakfast and she seems none the worse for her fright last night. Her husband insisted that I remain through the morning, however, in case I was needed."

Trenholm looked around at Alan. "What has become of Nash?"

"I haven't the faintest idea," roughly. "I keep out of his way."

"Why?" The question shot from Trenholm and Roberts glanced at him, his interest instantly aroused.

"He's the type I can't stand—oily, unctuous, bah!" Alan's temper had gained the upper hand. "A pious fraud!"

What reply his companions would have made, he never learned, for at that moment the portières were pulled aside to admit the lawyer from Washington.

"Monsieur Cocoron" was the best Pierre could do in pronouncing the name of Corcoran. The chauffeur had taken it upon himself to usher the lawyer into the house in the absence of Martha Corbin, the newcomer having rung the front door bell at the moment Pierre was alone in the kitchen.

Daniel Corcoran had known Alan Mason since his boyhood, Doctor Roberts was his family physician, and Guy Trenholm he had met numerous times when visiting Paul Abbott, Senior. The lawyer's usual cheery smile was absent as he shook hands with them.

"This is a shocking affair!" he said. "Shocking! Paul was a fine young man, with a brilliant career ahead of him. I cannot conceive of any one harboring enmity against him; he was such a likable chap. And to find him murdered here in his home!" Corcoran shook a bewildered head. "Have you any clue to his murderer, Trenholm? Any later news than that published in the morning paper?"

Not only the lawyer waited expectantly for the sheriff's answer; Alan's eyes were glued to him, and Roberts also was giving him undivided attention; but Trenholm's expression told them nothing.

"The murder is still shrouded in mystery, Mr. Corcoran," he replied quietly. "We expected you here for the funeral yesterday."

Corcoran's face clouded over. "I was in Richmond and reached Washington late in the evening. I telegraphed my clerk to take Paul's will out of my office vault and bring it to the house this morning. I have it here," tapping his brief case. He turned to Alan. "Did I understand correctly from the papers that Mrs. Nash and her niece, Miss Elizabeth Carter, are staying here?"

"Yes," replied Alan, looking at him in some surprise.

"Very well; then please ask them to be present at the reading of the will. And, eh," looking about him, "do you prefer to have the reading take place here?"

Alan hesitated and glanced questioningly at Trenholm. "How about it?" he asked.

"This is all right," agreed Trenholm. "Will you ask Miss Carter to join us, Alan? I must speak to one of my men," and the sheriff unceremoniously opened one of the doors leading into the garden and walked around the house.

"Don't forget Mrs. Nash," called out Corcoran, as Alan hurried into the dining room.

"She is ill in bed," hastily broke in Roberts, as Alan paused in uncertainty at the lawyer's hail.

"Ah, then ask her husband to be present, if he is here," directed the lawyer. Corcoran moved over to a wicker table and Roberts helped him remove some magazines and books. Taking up his brief case, the former unlocked it, drew out a pad of blank paper, a pencil, and an official-looking document with an imposing seal. Without unfolding it, he put the document down in front of him and addressed Roberts.

"Paul was a queer character," he admitted. "In many ways a lovable fellow, with a curious, suspicious streak running through his make-up. In the last few years he has trusted no one—entirely."

Roberts' expression grew serious. "Cheerful and morose by turns," he said. "I never knew how I would find him, of late years—happy as a lark or down in the depths. I attribute it," he lowered his voice, "to shell-shock."

"It may be," agreed Corcoran. "But you recall his mother. Ah, here is Miss Carter," as Betty appeared, dressed in black, "and Dr. Nash." The lawyer shook hands with them gravely. "Now, if you will select chairs we will go ahead with the reading of Mr. Abbott's will. Alan," as the latter made a belated appearance, "ask Mr. Trenholm to come back."

Betty had selected a chair near the entrance to the library and out of the direct sunlight. From where she sat she caught a glimpse through the portières of Trenholm standing talking to a man. He advanced with Alan a moment later and entering the sunparlor, closed not only the portières but the folding doors as well.

Corcoran waited until every one was seated, then took a chair himself, and, picking up the will, put on his eyeglasses.

"This," he said, holding up the document so all might see the seal, "is the last will and testament of Paul Mason Abbott, duly executed in my office on July 23, 1922, six months ago, and witnessed by responsible persons, whose names are attached hereto." He cleared his throat. "The will reads as follows:

"IN THE NAME OF GOD, AMEN. I, Paul Mason Abbott, being of sound mind, and residing at Abbott's Lodge, Hills Bridge, Prince Georges County, Maryland, do declare this to be my last will and testament.

"I give and bequeath to Alan Mason, my cousin and only near relation, $500 in liberty bonds and the burial ground, known as the Mason Plot, adjacent to my estate of Abbott's Lodge.

"To my good friend and physician, Doctor William Roberts of Washington, $5,000. To my neighbor, Guy Trenholm of Upper Marlboro, the valuable hunting prints which he so often admired, a sapphire and diamond scarf-pin, and $25,000.

"To Mrs. Nash, for much kindness and hospitality shown me, my silver service, bearing the crest of the Abbotts.

"To Martha and Charles Corbin, for their faithful service to my father, I give the sum of $1,000 each, and permission to live, rent free, in the gardener's cottage at Abbott's Lodge, for the rest of their natural lives.

"To my fiancée, Miss Elizabeth Carter of Washington, I bequeath Abbott's Lodge, and the real and personal estate, not otherwise specified, of which I die possessed.

"Should Miss Carter marry after my death, my special bequest to her stands revoked, and Alan Mason will become my residuary legatee, provided he is married before my death. If such is not the case, then all my property, as above specified, is to revert to the State of Maryland and Abbott's Lodge be made a convalescent hospital for disabled American soldiers and a fund provided for its upkeep, and administered by officials appointed by the Governor of Maryland.

"I hereby appoint Daniel Corcoran of Washington my executor, and I charge him to see that all my just debts are paid out of my estate before it is divided.

"(Signed) PAUL MASON ABBOTT."

Witnesses. { "John Harbin, Marshall Turner, George Flint."

Absolute silence followed the reading of the will. Corcoran laid it down and took several papers out of his brief case.

"I have here a complete list of Paul Abbott's real estate holdings, investments and securities," he stated. "Roughly, his estate is estimated at a little over one million dollars."

Trenholm broke the thunderstruck silence.

"Great Scott!" he exclaimed, and involuntarily his eyes traveled to Betty Carter and Alan Mason. The latter was leaning against the door, looking dazedly at the little lawyer. Betty had risen and Corcoran, catching her glance, addressed her. He was a trifle confused by her expression and hastened to adjust his glasses that he might see her more distinctly.

"Paul Abbott loved you devotedly," he said, "as you can judge from his will."

"Love?" Betty could hardly articulate; her eyes were dark with passion. "Love, did you say? That is a will of *hate*," and before any one could stop her she had flung open the folding doors and darted into the dining room.

CHAPTER XV
THREE BEEHIVES

MIRIAM looked at her watch—two o'clock. The brilliant sunlight and the out of doors exerted an appeal she could not resist. Stopping only long enough to put on her hat and coat, she started down the corridor and, when passing Mrs. Nash's door, paused irresolutely. Mrs. Nash had recovered, when she left her at eight o'clock that morning, from her fright at discovering the disguised man in her room, but Miriam was troubled about her heart condition. She felt that she should speak to Somers before she went for her walk. She had told the maid to call her at any time if she needed assistance. If Mrs. Nash was asleep she could slip out without disturbing her.

Miriam softly turned the knob of the door and pushed it gently open, intending to beckon to Somers to come into the hall. She had opened it but a few inches when she heard Alexander Nash address his wife.

"I have just received a telegram from Canada, Dora," he said, and added more quickly as his wife looked up, a question on her lips, "from Frank Chisholm telling me of the sudden death of Boris Zybinn."

Mrs. Nash's reply was unheard by Miriam. She leaned limply against the doorjamb, her strength stricken from her. Their voices sounded far distant—unreal. It was fully two minutes before her brain cleared and she had a realizing sense of what Nash was saying.

"A remarkable will," he commented. "Alan receives practically nothing from his cousin, while Guy Trenholm is given twenty-five thousand dollars, a scarf-pin, and those wonderful old hunting prints. It is really extraordinary."

Miriam waited to hear no more. Closing the door as softly as she had opened it, she stole back to her room, unlocked her bag, and drew from it the letter she had found in Mrs. Nash's bedroom the night before. For a time she stood quite still, balancing the unopened letter in her hand; once she took up a hairpin, then laid it down, unused. Boris Zybinn! She shook her head and glanced about as if awakening from a nightmare.

A sound of voices coming through her open window caused her to look outside. Anna, her work done for the time being, was, as she expressed it to Martha later, "joshing" one of the constable's assistants—a young deputy whose susceptible heart had made him a willing victim to her wiles. The deputy's presence gave Miriam a sudden idea. Carefully placing the unopened letter in her hand bag, she went downstairs and hastened through the dining room, intending to go out of the door of the sunparlor and from there to the back of the house.

Martha—a rejuvenated Martha—looked up from changing the tablecloth at her approach, and Miriam, in spite of her absorption in her own affairs, noticed her changed appearance.

"Have ye heard, Miss—Ma'am," she began incoherently. "Mr. Paul, God rest his soul, has left me and Charles one thousand dollars each."

"Is that so? I congratulate you, Martha." Miriam shifted her hand bag and held it more firmly against her. There was an intangible something about Martha which invited distrust. "Mr. Abbott was most generous."

"Yes Miss—Ma'am; he had call to be," Martha's voice had assumed its old complaining whine. "Us took good care of him. I don't mind telling you Miss—Ma'am, that my husband ain't quite satisfied. He wants more."

"Oh!"

"Yes." Martha's grievances were displacing her first feeling of elation at the, to her, large sum of money. "Charles, he's mad, clean through. He says he's goin' to Sheriff Trenholm."

"And why to the Sheriff?" questioned Miriam in surprise.

"Oh, he's kinder good at giving advice—when ye got something to tell him." Martha's slow, expressive wink annoyed Miriam and without paying further attention to the woman, she went through the sunparlor and outside the house.

Martha, in no wise disturbed by Miriam's cool reception of her confidences, went slowly on with her work, her mental process of "thinking" betrayed by her facial contortions.

The young deputy was just starting his engine when Miriam appeared at the side of his car.

"Can you tell me where I will find Sheriff Trenholm?" she asked.

Ben Riley touched his hat and a pleased smile stole over his freckled face. He had admired Miriam at a distance for several days, although she had been utterly oblivious of his existence. That she might be under surveillance never entered her head. The indefatigable Martha had complained to her of the presence about Abbott's Lodge of a number of deputies, and Riley had been pointed out to her by Somers as one of them.

"The sheriff's at his home," Riley explained, then, as her face showed plainly her disappointment, he added, "Can I take a message to him? I'm on my way there now."

With Miriam to think was to act. It was imperative that she see Trenholm.

"Can I drive over with you?" she asked, and her charming smile completed Riley's conquest.

"Yes, Miss Ward," he stammered, with gratifying emphasis, and opened the door of his roadster. "Hop in."

They had gone half the distance to Upper Marlboro and were about to turn from the main road to the one leading to Trenholm's bungalow, when they were passed by Mrs. Nash's Rolls-Royce which continued down the main road at such a speed that Miriam had only a glimpse of Alexander Nash seated by the chauffeur. The fur collar of Pierre's heavy chauffeur's overcoat was turned up about his face and his most intimate friend would have failed to recognize him as he drove along, under Nash's instructions, breaking the speed laws of Maryland.

Pablo, the Filipino, answered Miriam's ring of the door bell at the bungalow with a promptness that suggested that he had observed Riley's car when it turned into the driveway.

"Come inside, Mees," he said with hospitable intent. "My master will return in one little moment. He is in de garage and I will go at once and tell him that you are here. It is cold, yes?" as the rising wind blew the daily papers off the hall table. He closed the door with alacrity and led the way into the library. "Sit down, Mees, and be comfortable."

Miriam hardly noticed his departure. The long drive over had brought reflection in its train and she was regretting her hasty action. She glanced about the library, taking in, as Alan had done the night before, its suggestion of cultivation, its homelike atmosphere. Guy Trenholm's personality permeated the room. She did not sit down, as Pablo had suggested, but remained by the table in deep thought, and Trenholm, about to enter the room, stopped in the doorway and studied her intently. The proud poise of her head, her becoming toque, her plain, but well-fitting coat, her vivid coloring, made more brilliant by her drive in the wind, all were a fitting complement to the setting in which she stood. Trenholm caught his breath and his heart beat more quickly, but his expression and voice conveyed no feeling beyond a courteous welcome as he stepped forward to greet her.

"Won't you sit down?" he asked, pulling forward a chair. "I am sorry to have kept you waiting. Let me help you with your coat."

Miriam thanked him, then sat down and waited for him to take the chair opposite hers. As he looked at her inquiringly, she came directly to the point. Opening her hand bag, she took out the letter bearing the Canadian postage and held it up.

"I found this letter," she said, "when on duty last night. It was tucked in one of the chairs in Mrs. Nash's bedroom. I bring it to you as I found it—unopened."

Trenholm took the letter from her outstretched hand, and turned it over several times before making any comment.

"And what is there about the letter to have attracted your attention, Miss Ward?" he finally asked, and wondered at the look in her eyes.

"The seal," she said simply. "It matches this," and she drew out of her bag the half-burnt envelope and turned it over so that he could view the flap with its black crest. "It is that crest of which you found drawings in my bag."

"Yes, I recognize the three beehives," he replied. Leaning back in his chair he reached over and took up a heavy volume from a smoking stand where he had flung it earlier that day. "I borrowed this book on heraldry from the Congressional Library," he explained, and turned the leaves with lightning rapidity until he found the page he wished. "See, the three beehives," pointing to a fine colored engraving, "and the proud motto of the Paltoffs of Russia—'Always without Fear.'"

Miriam stared at the printed page and then at Trenholm, and respect and admiration were in her glance.

"That was clever of you," she exclaimed. "So you guess—"

"Much," quietly, "except your connection with the Paltoffs."

Miriam looked about the library. There was no likelihood of their conversation being interrupted.

"Dmitri Paltoff, Grand Maitre de la Cour, married my aunt," she said simply. "He was the last of his race, and when he was killed, the right to use that crest died with him. Its use on these envelopes was consequently a shock, and aroused my keenest interest at once, for"—she hesitated and spoke more slowly—"this black crest has a peculiar indentation and varies in no particular from the seal on my uncle's watch fob, which I saw snatched from his dying grasp by a Bolshevik in Vladivostok."

Trenholm was regarding her with absorbed interest. "So that was it," he murmured, then raised his voice slightly. "Do you, by chance, know the Bolshevik who took the seal?"

"Yes. It was my uncle's secretary, Boris Zybinn." Miriam leaned forward in her earnestness. "Just before I left Abbott's Lodge, I accidentally overheard Doctor Nash tell his wife that he had a telegram from Canada stating that Boris had died suddenly."

Trenholm stared at her a moment. Rising with some abruptness, he went over to the wall, touched a concealed spring and one of the wooden panels slid aside and revealed the door of a small safe. When he came back and resumed his old seat, he carried a package of letters.

"I watched you when you glanced over these letters," he confessed, "in the hall at Abbott's Lodge. And I have read them a dozen times trying to find out what there was about them which claimed such interest on your part."

"I was looking for the black crest," she admitted. "You see the envelopes are identical with this burnt one," holding it up again. "I did not open any of the letters. Who wrote them?"

"They are signed by Boris Zybinn," Trenholm opened several and laid them in her lap. "Do you recognize the handwriting?"

She shook her head. "No. Boris was clever; he might easily have learned to disguise his writing. He was an excellent linguist, as most Russians are. What was he doing in Canada?"

"Gentleman farming," answered Trenholm. "He had a place outside of Toronto and adjoining Doctor Nash's country estate. It was while visiting Nash that Paul Abbott and he became acquainted."

"And these letters, what are they about?" questioned Miriam eagerly.

"Farming," briefly. "And nothing else. Paul wished to model his place here after Zybinn's, especially his fruit orchard. I suppose that he kept them, for reference," and Trenholm tossed the remaining letters on his desk table which stood almost at Miriam's elbow.

Miriam drew back in bitter disappointment. "And that is all," she exclaimed. "I have indeed found a mare's nest."

"As far as the letters go," agreed Trenholm, with characteristic frankness. "But there is another matter of vital importance," he glanced carefully about the room, sprang up and closed both of the doors, one of which led into the main hall and the other into a smaller room, where he generally conducted business. When he came back to Miriam he moved his chair closer to her side. "You know of the Paltoff diamond?" he asked.

"Yes. I have heard its history often from my uncle," she replied. "It was given by one of his ancestors to Peter the Great."

"To purchase royal favor," supplemented Trenholm "And forms one of the Crown jewels."

"You are wrong," she corrected him swiftly. "It is not a Crown jewel, but it has always been in the possession of the reigning Czar, handed down from father to son."

"And where is it now, Miss Ward?" The swift question took her unawares and she grew pale.

"I do not know," she stated, and her eyes did not falter before his searching glance. "Frankly, I do not know its present whereabouts."

"There is a rumor that it was smuggled out of Russia." Trenholm never took his eyes from her. "Can you tell me if that is true?"

She did not at once reply and he did not hurry her. "Why do you ask?" she demanded finally. "What is your interest in the Paltoff diamond?"

"This!" Trenholm opened his leather wallet and took from it a folded note. "Read it."

Slowly Miriam took in the sense of the written sentence:

Let him who hopes to solve the mystery of Paul Abbott's death find the lost Paltoff jewel.

"What!" She half rose from her chair, then dropped back again. Her face was ghastly and Trenholm watched her in growing concern. "Who wrote this note?"

"I do not know. I found it in the pocket of my overcoat when I returned from Paul's funeral." Trenholm paused. "The handwriting is unfamiliar."

He doubted if Miriam heard his last sentence; she kept so quiet, so immovable. Suddenly she pressed her fingers to her eyes and when she took them away, the lids were wet. She looked at him long and searchingly. Could she trust him? She *must*—there was no other course open to her.

"I will tell you in confidence what I know of the Paltoff diamond," she said. "But you must pledge me your word not to repeat it."

"I give you my word," Trenholm held out his hand, and as she felt his strong, steady clasp her heart lightened and her sense of utter loneliness grew less.

"I will be as brief as possible." She paused to clear her throat of a suspicious lump. "My father, John Ward of Indianapolis, was in the Diplomatic service, and stationed for a long time in Russia, where we lived with my aunt and her husband. After father's death, mother and I came to New York. She was a great invalid and did not long survive him." She stumbled in her speech and stopped, and Trenholm gave her a moment to collect herself.

"Yes?" he prompted gently. "Continue."

"Mother died just before the outbreak of the World War," she went on. "It was necessary for me to find employment and I decided to become a nurse. I trained at St. Luke's Hospital and went overseas at once upon graduation. It would be too long to tell you of my experiences, but finally I reached Russia and saw service in the hospitals there. Then came the revolution." She drew in her breath sharply. "God! The horrors that we lived through—the Bolsheviki were fiends in human form!"

"And the Paltoff diamond?" he asked.

"Oh, the diamond." She collected herself. "My uncle was for years Grand Master of the Imperial Court and trusted absolutely by the Czar. Just before he was made prisoner, the Czar took from the hilt of his dress sword, worn only on state occasions, the Paltoff diamond, and charged Uncle Dmitri, on his fealty to the Crown, to smuggle it out of Russia, and raise money upon it so that, should the Imperial family have to flee, something might be saved for them."

"What happened next?" demanded Trenholm as she paused.

Miriam sighed. "My uncle saw his gallant son crucified before his eyes; his daughters, taken prisoners with other ladies of the Court, were transported by steamer to a loathsome prison. Before the vessel docked they threw themselves into the sea, oh, gladly"—she added, seeing Trenholm's expression—"for the captain and his crew forced them to leave their cabin doors unlocked at night." She paused and put her hands before her eyes. When she looked up, Trenholm saw tragedy mirrored in their dark depths.

"With other refugees Uncle Dmitri and I finally reached Vladivostok, in rags and our money gone. Oh, Mr. Trenholm, pray God that you may never know what starvation is!" She stopped to control her voice. "We lived in a hovel in the filthiest part of the city. I had lost my passport or it had been stolen from me. I applied to the American consul—he promised help but none came."

"Poor girl!" Trenholm took her hand and pressed it warmly. "Would you rather stop?"

"No. Uncle Dmitri still had the Paltoff diamond and despite our agony would not part with it. When we dared to talk, for spies were all around us, we tried to plan to get the jewel safely out of Russia, even if we ourselves failed to reach the United States." Miriam stopped to clear her throat, for her voice had grown husky with emotion.

"One morning I was half delirious from hunger and privation, when Uncle Dmitri came inside the hovel followed by a man," she continued. "He crawled over to the straw on which I lay and told me that his companion was an American soldier who had saved his life in a brawl with drunken peasants. He feared that he had been recognized as Paltoff, the trusted friend of the Czar."

"I see," broke in Trenholm. "What next?"

"Our plight was desperate and my uncle took the American into his confidence, and the latter agreed to carry the diamond to the United States, provided he could smuggle it aboard the transport." She sighed deeply. "I was too ill to follow all that was said, but uncle took the diamond from its hiding place and the American sat down near me and unwound a bandage from about a wound in the calf of his leg. At his direction I opened the wound, placed the diamond inside it, and, having a surgeon's field service kit which a doctor, like ourselves a refugee, had left in the hovel the day before, I sutured the wound and replaced the bandages."

Trenholm stared at her. "American brains and pluck!" he exclaimed, and the admiration in his voice brought the swift color to her white cheeks.

"The American had not been gone five minutes before Boris Zybinn came in, followed by a swarm of the Bolsheviki," she went on, keeping her voice steady by an effort of will only, as the tragic scene rose vividly before her. "A whisper had gotten around that Uncle Dmitri had the Paltoff diamond. They put him to torture and he died as a brave man should, without fear and without betraying the Czar's trust."

"And you? What did they do to you?" demanded Trenholm, his usually calm tones betraying interest at fever heat.

"The American consul came in time to save me from all but this." Drawing back her sleeve she showed a brand burned into the soft white flesh. "Thank God! I had the strength to tell Boris nothing of the diamond."

Trenholm leaned forward impulsively. "I'd like to shake hands with you," he said, and the strong clasp of his fingers made her wince. There was a brief pause before he asked: "And the name of the American soldier?"

Miriam drew from around her neck a gold chain from which hung a locket. Opening it she took out a tiny soiled paper.

"The soldier wrote down his name and address and handed it to Uncle Dmitri," she explained. "But Boris got there before he could give it to me and it was torn up—all but this."

Trenholm looked long and carefully at the one letter on the paper.

"'M'," he repeated. "'M'—it is Paul Abbott's peculiar formation of his middle initial. I have seen it too often to be mistaken. And Paul Abbott, I know, saw service with the A.E.F. in Vladivostok."

———————————————

CHAPTER XVI
THE THIRTEENTH LETTER

GUY TRENHOLM raised his head. "May I keep this little paper in my safe?" he asked, taking it up. "I will return it at any time should you require it."

Miriam snapped her locket shut and slipped it inside her gown.

"The paper is far safer with you than with me," she replied, and sat quietly in her chair until Trenholm returned from placing it in a compartment of his safe. "It is incredible that Paul Abbott should have been the American soldier to whom Uncle Dmitri intrusted the diamond."

"But not impossible," retorted Trenholm. "And the law of chance brought you to his bedside just before his death. How was it you failed to recognize him?"

"I never really saw the American soldier's face." She sat back in a more comfortable position, conscious, for the first time, of complete fatigue. Recounting the tragic death of her Russian relatives and her own suffering, even to Trenholm's sympathetic ears, was a severe strain. "We had no window in our hovel; only the faint light from a candle. I believe he wore a beard, but I was too ill to care, at the moment, what he looked like. My uncle trusted him and that was enough. Five years have passed since then."

"I understand," exclaimed Trenholm sympathetically, then with a tenaciousness which was part of the man, he added: "Was there nothing familiar about Paul's appearance?"

She shook her head. "No. I have no doubt that illness had changed his appearance, Mr. Trenholm, to some extent. But with the Paltoff diamond far from my thoughts, and looking upon Mr. Abbott simply as a patient, if he had seemed even vaguely familiar I would have attributed it to the same feeling one has in passing a stranger in the street whom one might have met somewhere. You know the sensation."

Trenholm nodded in agreement. "Have you made no effort to trace the Paltoff diamond?"

"I was desperately ill for months, Mr. Trenholm; and it was fully a year before I regained anything like my old strength. There was no one I could rely upon—no one in whom I had confidence. I tried, however, to interest one man, a lawyer," her lips tightened, "that experience taught me a lesson I shall never forget." She turned scarlet and for the first time dropped her eyes before Trenholm's glance. She missed the sudden hot wrath which kindled in his eyes; a second later and he had himself in hand again.

"Can you describe the diamond, Miss Ward?" he asked. "And tell me its value?"

"It is a diamond of astonishing purity, of about forty-nine carats, and has an extraordinary play and brilliance," answered Miriam. "Though much smaller in size than other world-famous diamonds, it is claimed by experts to be an absolutely flawless gem. I believe it is worth in the neighborhood of $200,000 and possibly more."

A low whistle escaped Trenholm. "A frightful invitation to crime!" he ejaculated.

"And Boris Zybinn was in Canada and in communication with Paul Abbott," pointed out Miriam slowly. "Mr. Trenholm, I know a little of the evil accomplished by that renegade Russian. There is some significance in those letters of his to Mr. Abbott, innocent as they may appear. I will *never* believe otherwise!"

Trenholm leaned forward and, picking up the letters, laid them in Miriam's hands. "Read them over carefully," he begged. "I am open to conviction. But look here, Miss Ward, why didn't Zybinn come down to Abbott's Lodge and visit Paul and then steal the diamond? He might have done that without arousing suspicion. Why write letters about it?"

"Possibly he feared arrest and extradition for a former crime if he came into the United States," suggested Miriam, and Trenholm straightened up abruptly.

"There may be something in that idea," he admitted. "Read the letters aloud, Miss Ward."

Obediently Miriam opened first one and then another. Except for the precision of the language used, none were out of the ordinary. Each letter began: "My dear Abbott," and closed with the conventional, "Yours sincerely," and the signature, "Boris Zybinn." The contents of each referred only to agriculture. Miriam dropped the last one in her lap with a despondent gesture; then her expression brightened.

"You haven't looked at the unopened letter," she exclaimed. "See, you have left it there on the table."

Trenholm picked up the envelope and examined it carefully. "It is just like the others in appearance," he declared. "It must have come several days before Paul's murder," examining the postmark. "Corbin, however, can answer that question."

"I wonder why Mr. Abbott did not read it?"

"Too ill, perhaps—especially if he judged the letter unimportant."

Trenholm hunted about on his table until he found a letter opener and, using it dextrously, succeeded in raising the flap without breaking the seal. Taking care not to crease or otherwise mar the envelope, he drew out the folded sheet and read aloud the brief message it contained:

SUNNYMEADE FARM
TORONTO, CANADA
January 22, 1923

DEAR ABBOTT:

Sorry to learn that you are not well. Perhaps a change may do you good. Why not run up here for a week or two? I will be very happy to put you up if the Nashs are not at their place.

Chisholm says the two grays are seventeen hands and entirely sound. Would advise offer of a thousand for the pair.

Yours in haste,
BORIS ZYBINN.

Trenholm tossed down the letter in disgust. "Nothing to that!" he exclaimed. "They have fine horses in Canada, and Paul purchased several last year, and sold them at a good figure to one of our neighbors. What is it, Miss Ward?" observing her changed expression.

Without answering, Miriam pulled her chair around so that she sat facing the table. Picking up the letters she spread each one, with its envelope, before her, and slowly counted them.

"Eleven," she explained, "and this burnt envelope is twelve, and this last letter makes a total of thirteen *unimportant* letters."

"What then?" asked Trenholm, struck by her manner. Going around the table he stood looking over her shoulder.

"Have you noticed the postage?" she queried.

"Surely. They are Canadian stamps."

"Isn't postage from Canada three cents for first-class mail?"

"Yes."

"Then why does each letter bear *five one-cent* stamps?" glancing swiftly upward. "Boris Zybinn must have known the correct postage required."

"Perhaps he thought that his letters weighed more than one ounce."

"If so, the postage would have been double, or *six* cents," she remarked quickly. "Five cents would not have covered it. Besides, I don't believe that one of these letters weighs over an ounce."

Trenholm reached over and picked up his letter scales. "Try one," he suggested, and, as she did so, "Not quite one ounce. Try the next."

Miriam laid each letter on the scales, first putting it back in its proper envelope; not one was above one ounce in weight!

"They all come under the three-cent postage rate," she exclaimed. "Any one writing as many as thirteen letters to one correspondent would have found out that fact, especially a person living in Canada."

Trenholm considered Miriam and then the letters in silence for a minute. Picking up the thirteenth letter, which Miriam had brought to him unopened that afternoon, he took out the sheet of paper and held the envelope up to the light and studied it intently. As he lowered it, Miriam caught sight of his face and sprang to her feet.

"You have found something?"

"Yes, thanks to your persistency!" And she colored warmly at the enthusiasm in his voice and manner. "See here!" and Trenholm again held the envelope up to the light and at an angle so that she could see it as well as he. "The edges of the stamps appear cut in a wedge shape in certain places, and there are several pinholes through two of the stamps. The cuts do not appear to result from the careless tearing off of the stamps from the sheet, and consequent damage to the perforations, but are apparently made with scissors."

"You are right," agreed Miriam. "And when the letter has no light behind it, they do not show at all against the white ground of the envelope. Is it a code?"

Trenholm twirled his mustache in perplexity. "The cuts appear at irregular intervals," he replied. "They seem to be hastily made and are not absolutely uniform. I wonder—" he broke off abruptly, stood in thought for several seconds, then going over to the book shelves which lined one of the walls, searched about until he located several books and carried them back to the table where Miriam stood examining the thirteenth envelope.

"Strangely enough," he explained, "Paul's father gave me his stamp collection—a fine one—as Paul never had the craze for collecting stamps even as a boy, and being a human magpie I keep everything bestowed upon me," with a quick boyish smile which softened wonderfully his usually self-repressed expression. "I hope luck is with me and I still have tucked inside one of these albums a perforation gauge."

"A what?"

"Perforations, Miss Ward, have a definite position on each stamp with relation to one another, though they may be irregular on two separate stamps," went on Trenholm. "In other words, the distance between perforations is always the same, though they may vary a fractional part of a line in their position at the corners."

"And the gauge," she prompted, as he paused.

"Is used to measure the number of perforations to the inch," Trenholm spoke slowly, to be sure that she understood his meaning. "By applying a perforation gauge to the edge of a stamp, if the position of one perforation is known, that of all the others will be indicated."

Trenholm paused and opened one of the stamp albums. He turned the pages rapidly, and found the stamp he wanted, but no gauge. Taking up the other album he shook it over the table. A small shower of loose stamps, several odd envelopes and a piece of bristol board fell on the table. With a relieved exclamation, Trenholm clutched the perforation gauge, brushing the stamps aside.

"Here is a Canadian stamp of the same issue," he said. "Paul wrote me when he was last in Canada, and I kept the stamp. Let's see—"

Miriam waited with absorbed attention while he applied the gauge to the stamp. When he looked up his eyes were shining.

"The stamp has exactly fifty-two perforations," he announced. "Can it be a coincidence or a—"

"A what?"

He looked at her without speaking for a moment. "The number is just twice that of the letters of the alphabet." Trenholm drew in his breath. "I have come to your way of thinking, Miss Ward. It must be a code, and it may be that two alphabets are registered on each stamp, the cuts corresponding to the letters according to the number of the particular perforation affected, counting from one corner of the stamp."

Miriam, who had been following his explanation with close attention, nodded her head wisely.

"I see," she broke in. "That would explain any irregularity in the cuts, because for coding it would be sufficient to indicate the perforation intended to be cut, without making a mark of a definite character, and with this gauge of yours the number of the perforation which has been cut would be recognized at once."

"Exactly," he answered. "Without a gauge there would be great difficulty in determining the number of the perforation, because the cut might seem to create new indentations if carelessly made." Trenholm stopped and took up the envelope of the thirteenth letter and applied his gauge to the left-hand stamp, and Miriam, pencil in hand, assisted him.

Trenholm counted clockwise. "Five perforations are damaged," he declared, "numbers 8, 20, 23, 27, 30. Now, if the code is based on a double alphabet, these would become 8, 20, 23, 1, 3, or the letters H, T, W, A, C. How are the letters to be arranged, Miss Ward?"

She looked at her pad, where she had jotted down the letters as well as the figures. "There is only one vowel," she said. "It must be one word. Then why use two alphabets?"

"Possibly because of the accidental chance that the stamp perforations count up to fifty-two," replied Trenholm. "It would be convenient, in case of a word with many letters, to prevent destroying the appearance of the stamp by cutting too many indentations close to one another. Have you solved the first word?" as she checked an exclamation.

"Yes—'watch.'"

"Good!" Trenholm's eyes were bright with excitement. Looking again at the first stamp, he noticed that the first, third, and fifth letters of the words "watch" were indicated on the first alphabet, and the remaining letters on the second one.

Trenholm held up the envelope to the light again. "See, Miss Ward!" he exclaimed. "The stamp on the extreme right has only four indentations, though the left-hand corner has been cut off."

She studied the envelope in silence for a few seconds. "The letters are G and E in the first alphabet," she pointed out. "They must be the odd letters of the word coded, and R and V in the second alphabet, corresponding to the even letters, but I can't make any word out of them."

"Suppose we call the cut of the left-hand corner of the stamp an A," suggested Trenholm. "It may be a quick way to mark an indentation when a corner square was involved; though better care was used in the A of the second alphabet in the first stamp examined. What word have you now, Miss Ward?"

"Grave."

Trenholm stared at her. "Grave," he repeated, then, suppressing comment, went ahead decoding the message. "This center one appears the simplest," he said. "Here the perforations cut are numbers 5, 12, 20, 5, 18, 20—odd letters, E, L, T; even letters, E, R, T. Got them down, Miss Ward?"

"They make the word—letter," briefly, not glancing up. "Go ahead."

"The next letters are E, I, T, for the odd, and E, H, N, R, for the even." Trenholm laid down his perforation gauge and frowned. "The code seems to fail here," he grumbled. "It has given four even letters and only three odd. The other way around would be all right, but it is impossible to make a word with more even than odd letters."

"Let me see the envelope." Miriam put aside her pencil and carefully examined the stamps against the light. "Look, Mr. Trenholm, here are pinholes opposite some of the letters—two opposite the odd T, and one opposite the even H."

"Probably they stand for repetitions of the same letters, in which case the letters would be: odd—E, I, T, T, T; even—E, H, H, N, R," declared Trenholm. "But they don't make sense." He paused and looked at the stamps already decoded. "See here, the first letter in each word we have deciphered is on the side of the stamp which faces the left side of the envelope."

"Oh, then that accounts for the apparently careless manner in which the stamps are stuck on the envelope," said Miriam. "The only letter on the second stamp, which is indicated by a cut in the way you have just described, is T."

"So our next word begins with T." Trenholm took up a pencil and did some figuring on Miriam's pad. "With so many T's and H's to use, suppose we start off with Th," he began, "and the next letter is either E, I, or T. It must be one of the vowels. No, E is no good." Trenholm ran his fingers through his hair until it stood upright. "We'll take I, and here is an R available—by Jove—*thirteenth*!"

"So it is!" Miriam's excitement was rising. "The words we have so far are, 'watch thirteenth letter——grave.'"

"Now for the last stamp!" Trenholm took up gauge and pencil. "The odd letters are E, two I's, one indicated by another pinhole, and S. The even letters are C, D, S, U. The position of the stamp shows that the first letter is S. Of the four even letters available for the next position, only the vowel can be used, making Su." Trenholm paused and wrote rapidly several combinations of the available letters, then looked up with a low exclamation—"Suicides."

"And the completed message then stands—'Watch thirteenth letter suicides grave,'" repeated Miriam. "What do you make of it, Mr. Trenholm?"

"Nothing—now," he admitted frankly. "We know the code. Help me decipher these other eleven envelopes and the burnt one. Fortunately the stamps on it are intact."

Half an hour later Miriam and Trenholm sat back in their chairs and looked at each other. The latter took up one of the pads they had used.

"Here are the thirteen decoded messages, of five words each, concealed in the stamps on the thirteen envelopes," he stated. "Listen carefully, Miss Ward, and tell me what you make of them."

Fear Paul suspicious of Betty.
Unwise to trust her judgment.
Judge her influence is waning.
Is there any other woman?
Last interview with Paul disastrous.
He declines to return jewel.
Do not lose your nerve.
Believe he can prove nothing.
Does not guess your motive.
Situation growing tense; money required.
Learned hiding place changed often.
Next time can tell definitely.
Watch thirteenth letter; suicides grave.

Miriam wrinkled her forehead in deep thought. "For whom were those messages intended, Mr. Trenholm?" she asked.

"For the man who later killed Paul Abbott," he replied quietly.

"And he—"

"Is some one who was with Paul and had access to his mail, and so could read the code on these apparently innocent letters." Trenholm rose suddenly and looked down at her. "It was a devilish scheme and devilishly carried out."

"By Boris Zybinn's confederate." Miriam also rose. "Have you any idea who that confederate is?"

Absently Trenholm took up his pipe and fingered it. "Some one who knew Paul intimately," he said. "And who has been with him during the past few months, for the dates on these letters cover that period of time. But as to his identity—the coded messages give no clue."

"That is true," agreed Miriam. "Another question—When he murdered Paul Abbott did he secure the Paltoff diamond?"

Trenholm had located his tobacco pouch and filled his pipe mechanically, his thoughts elsewhere.

"Frankly," he said slowly, "I am inclined to think he didn't."

CHAPTER XVII
CHERCHEZ LA FEMME

GUY TRENHOLM helped Miriam into his powerful roadster and then, with a murmured word of apology, slipped back into his bungalow. Miriam waited patiently, unmindful of his prolonged absence and thankful for the opportunity of rest undisturbed. Her ideas were confused—chaotic. The thirteen messages which she and Trenholm had just decoded were ringing in her head, but, try as she would, she could think of no solution to the enigma. The Law of Chance had indeed plunged her into an impenetrable mystery. Trenholm's voice at her elbow caused her to start slightly.

"I am extremely sorry to have been so long," he said, taking his place behind the steering wheel. "Pablo," to the Filipino, who had followed him from the front door and was clinging frantically to the collars of the police dogs in his endeavor to keep them out of the car, "let no one enter the house. If any one calls on the telephone, tell them I am at Abbott's Lodge."

The next instant the roadster had glided into the highway, and with Trenholm's impatient foot on the accelerator, was making record time in its dash for Abbott's Lodge.

Pablo was busy going about his work, whistling shrilly, when a heavy knock on the side door interrupted him. Answering it, he found a man in chauffeur's livery just about to implant a heavy kick on the panels by way of emphasis.

"Your mastair, where is he?" demanded Pierre, and Pablo's back stiffened at his insolent manner.

"None of your business," he retorted, and slammed the door. The heavy bombardment of knocks which followed was stopped by Alexander Nash's appearance on the scene. He had waited in the Nash limousine, but the sound of conflict stirred him to action. His voice, raised in anger, caused Pablo to glance through the pantry window, and at sight of the clergyman, he at once opened the side door.

"What is eet?" he asked blandly, ignoring Pierre utterly. "Did some one knock?"

"I wish to see Sheriff Trenholm at once," stated the clergyman. "Tell him that Doctor Nash is here."

"He is away."

"Oh!" Nash looked a trifle nonplussed, then asked briskly, "Where will I find him?"

Pablo paused, in his turn, for reflection. Trenholm had stated very clearly that should any one call him by telephone he, Pablo, was to say that he was to be found at Abbott's Lodge. Trenholm, however, had specified a telephone call only, and not a caller in person, therefore, according to Pablo's reasoning, he could not divulge the whereabouts of his master to Nash.

"He gone out," he replied, assuming a stupid air and lack of English, which he spoke remarkably well, except for a distinct accent. "No tell where go."

Nash's disappointment was obvious. "Think again!" he begged, and jingled some loose coins in his pocket suggestively. But Pablo's total lack of expression proved more exasperating than enlightening. "Come, where is the sheriff?"

"I dunno," Pablo shrugged. "Maybe he come back to dinner, maybe not. Want to wait in your car?"

"No, certainly not." Nash frowned thoughtfully. "Let me use your telephone a moment," and he held out a bank note.

Pablo backed away. "Sorry, can't use—" He got no further.

Pierre, with a dexterity which Pablo had not anticipated, had slipped between the Filipino and the open door, and, with a vigorous push, sent Pablo sprawling. But the latter was too quick for him. With a spring like a panther, Pablo was on his back and Pierre measured his length on the ground.

"Stop this unseemly brawling," commanded Nash, looking genuinely shocked. "Pierre, go at once to my car. As for you," turning to Pablo, who rose with reluctance and one final kick which sent the chauffeur's headgear down the path, "I shall report your conduct to Mr. Trenholm." And he stalked away.

Without giving a thought to Pablo's habit of taking everything he said literally, Trenholm slackened the roadster's speed when they got within a mile of Abbott's Lodge.

"Do you see very much of Miss Carter?" he asked.

"No. She is never with Mrs. Nash at night and I am not around the house in the daytime," replied Miriam. She hesitated perceptibly. "Betty is the only name given in the messages we decoded. Does it refer to Miss Carter?"

"To whom else could it refer?" and Miriam was silenced by his tone. She stole a look at Trenholm. She dared not admit, even to herself, how frequently her thoughts were centered on the self-contained man by her side.

"Miss Ward"—Trenholm drove the car to the side of the road and stopped—"did you catch sight of the man in Mrs. Nash's bedroom early this morning?"

Her answer was disappointing. "No. I was halfway up the staircase when I heard her cry out, but when I reached her she was alone in the room," she explained. "I had left the hall door partly open and found it practically in the same position upon my return."

Trenholm considered her answer for a second. When he addressed her again she was struck by the gravity of his tone.

"Exactly what is the matter with Mrs. Nash?" he inquired. "I am not asking from idle curiosity, Miss Ward," observing her hesitation, "but as an officer of the law."

Miriam eyed him in startled wonder. What did his question portend?

"Doctor Roberts told me he felt that he had not located the real trouble," she replied. "Nor can I give a reason for her, at times, alarming symptoms."

"Can you not venture an opinion?"

"Mr. Trenholm!"

He turned and his rare smile gave her a ray of comfort and a sense of security.

"It's unethical, I know," he said. "But you must realize, Miss Ward, that we are confronted with a dastardly conspiracy, the tentacles of which reach from Russia to Abbott's Lodge. Can I not count upon your aid to expose Zybinn's plot?"

"You can." Her voice rang out clearly, and again Trenholm smiled, well pleased. "I have sometimes thought that Mrs. Nash's condition is due to a heart depressant—"

"A coal-tar poison," quietly. "And by whom administered?"

Miriam moved unhappily. "I am not in the sickroom at all hours," she observed dryly. "Miss Carter is there during the day, and Doctor Nash spends much time with his wife."

Trenholm contemplated her, a gleam of something besides admiration in his eyes; then shifting his gears and releasing his brake, he drove onward.

"Do you recall the exact wording of the coded message in the thirteenth letter?" he asked, after a brief silence.

"Yes. It was: 'Watch thirteenth letter suicides grave,'" she looked at him inquiringly. "Does the word 'suicide' take the possessive 's', or is its meaning plural?"

"That remains to be seen." He turned the car into the driveway to Abbott's Lodge, and before stopping under the *porte cochère*, addressed her in a voice carefully lowered to reach her ear alone. "Say nothing of the thirteen letters to *any one.*"

"Of course not!"

He was quick to detect her hurt tone. "Forgive me," he begged, and his low, earnest voice impressed her. "I depend on your aid absolutely and trust you implicitly," then as she flashed a glance upward of glad relief, he added, "Don't forget those five words, for I firmly believe that the solution to Paul's mysterious murder rests in the thirteenth letter." Their approach had been seen from inside the Lodge and Corbin swung open the door. Trenholm had opportunity for only one hurried sentence, "The thirteenth letter," he repeated, under his breath, "of the alphabet is 'M.'"

Corbin favored Miriam with an unpleasant glance as she sped by him into the house, but touched his forehead, with some show of respect, to Trenholm.

"Mrs. Nash wishes to see ye," he stated. His shifty eyes fell before the sheriff's steady gaze. "Can I have a word with ye, sir; me and Martha—"

"Yes?" inquiringly, as the caretaker paused in uncertainty. "Well?"

Corbin licked his lips. Talking to the sheriff was not quite so easy a task as he had represented to Martha, and he instantly shifted the responsibility.

"Martha's dressin' now, sir; but she'll be down d'reckly," he mumbled. "An' before ye go, sir, please ask for her."

Trenholm took silent note of the man's twitching facial muscles and his unhealthy pallor.

"Very well," he said. "I will send for Martha. Wait—no, go on," as Corbin stopped reluctantly at the first injunction, and, giving Trenholm no time to reconsider his second order, he disappeared in the direction of the kitchen.

Trenholm hung up his hat and overcoat in the closet off the living room in deep thought. He had intended questioning Corbin as to the hours of receiving mail at Abbott's Lodge, but he shrewdly suspected that Martha would prove a more reliable source of information, and so dismissed the caretaker with the question unasked.

Trenholm's low tap on Mrs. Nash's bedroom door brought Somers in response. On recognizing the sheriff she drew back and held the door more widely open.

"My mistress is expecting you," she said. "Come in, sir."

It was the first time Mrs. Nash had met Guy Trenholm face to face, though each had had glimpses of the other during Mrs. Nash's occasional visits to Abbott's Lodge in the past. Under pretense of much languor, she was slow in offering him her hand and equally slow in releasing his. Trenholm's pressure on her icy fingers forced her rings into her flesh, but aside from a slight, very slight, intake of her breath, she gave no sign of how much he hurt her.

"Please take that chair," she said, as Somers, obedient to previous instructions, pushed forward the chair Miriam had occupied the night before and in which she had found the thirteenth letter. "You will fill it nicely, Mr. Trenholm; it is made for such big frames as you and my husband. I feel," she added as he kept a discreet silence, waiting for her to open the interview, "that you and I should be old acquaintances; I have heard so many nice things about you from both Paul and his father."

"Thank you, Mrs. Nash!" Trenholm sat back and eyed her gravely. Her rouge was cleverly applied and her hair was becomingly dressed. But to his critical mind there was something unnatural in the high notes of her voice, in the constant tremble of her hand, which, strive as she did, she could not control. "I have frequently hoped to meet you, and frankly"—with a disarming smile—"particularly after your experiences last night."

"You come directly to the point," she remarked. "I can only tell you that, after Miss Ward left me, I closed my eyes—for a few minutes only—and opened them to find the room in darkness, to feel some one creeping to my bedside, the touch of the beard on my hand—" The shrug of her shoulders was eloquent. "Have you, Sheriff Trenholm, discovered the identity of the intruder?"

He shook his head. "I must admit failure," he said. "Give me a little more time."

She frowned, then smiled, and Trenholm decided that a fiery temper was kept under iron control. "My husband has gone to employ a celebrated detective agency to solve the mystery," she stated. "I thought that you should know and so sent for you."

"Thank you," simply, and settling himself more comfortably in the big chair Trenholm awaited her next remark.

"You are not exactly loquacious," she commented dryly. "Have you been told the terms of Paul Abbott's will?"

"Yes. Your niece will inherit a very handsome fortune."

"Provided she remains single the rest of her natural life." Mrs. Nash's laugh smote unpleasantly on his ear. "Betty is so very young—not yet out of her twenties. Does wealth compensate, Mr. Trenholm, for a lonely old age?"

"To some natures it does." Trenholm's voice was softly modulated to suit a sick room, and Mrs. Nash had to listen attentively to catch every word he said. "It seems a pity that Paul and Miss Carter were not married before his death."

Mrs. Nash's eyelids flickered slightly; otherwise she regarded him with unchanged expression. "It is a pity," she agreed, "in a way. But I have no doubt that certain terms in Paul's ridiculous will can be set aside."

"Ah, on what grounds?"

"That he was not of sound mind when it was drawn up," quietly. "In view of the mystery surrounding Paul's shocking murder, Mr. Trenholm, I feel that you should be informed on certain matters."

"And what are they, Mrs. Nash?" as she paused. Trenholm was giving her flattering attention and she smiled shrewdly.

"My father had given his consent to Betty's engagement to Paul," she went on, "when, shortly after, we noticed a change in Paul. His morbid tendencies became more pronounced and he suffered from the delusion that people were pursuing him." She looked at Trenholm. "You know the unfortunate story of his mother?"

"That she died insane, yes."

"My father grew more and more distressed, for Betty is his only grandchild. At last my husband went to Doctor Roberts and asked him to join my father's party on our yachting trip to Bermuda, so that he might have Paul under mental observation." Mrs. Nash paused to clear her throat. "That was only two months ago."

"And what conclusion did Roberts come to regarding Paul's mental condition?" questioned Trenholm swiftly.

"Roberts is an old fogy!" For once Mrs. Nash's self-control slipped. She had herself in hand again before Trenholm could guess the cause of her emotion. "And his affection for Paul biased his judgment. My husband would have done better had he employed another physician."

Trenholm scrutinized her intently for several minutes. "And what connection is there between Paul's mental condition and his murder?" he asked finally.

"Suicide—"

Trenholm laughed outright. "An utterly unpractical theory, Mrs. Nash," he remarked, and the dryness of his tone brought the carmine to her cheeks under her rouge. "It was physically impossible for Paul to have stabbed himself." He rose without ceremony and stared openly about the big bedroom. "I've been in here often when Mr. Abbott, Sr., used it as a sitting room," he said, "and these are the hunting prints which Paul left me." He looked down at Mrs. Nash, a faint smile still lingering about his lips. "I want these prints awfully. Please don't contest Paul's will," and turning his back upon her, he walked leisurely across the room and examined them.

Mrs. Nash's emotions were too great to permit her clear vision and she failed to detect Trenholm when he quietly took down the sketch of neglected graves which hung where Miriam had seen it during her first vigil in the sick room. Slipping the small picture inside his pocket, he strolled back to the bed.

"Good-by, Mrs. Nash," he bowed courteously, then bent further down until his lips nearly touched her right ear. "I am not much of a doctor, but I am of the opinion that you can get up."

When Mrs. Nash recovered her breath only Somers was in the bedroom.

CHAPTER XVIII
THE DEATH CLUTCH

MIRIAM did not stay long in her bedroom after leaving Guy Trenholm in the hall of Abbott's Lodge talking to Corbin. She had thought at first of lying down for a little while, but she was too restless. A walk would quiet her nerves, and, if Mrs. Nash had a good night, she might have an opportunity of relaxing and thereby gain some rest before morning.

It took Miriam only a few minutes to put on her coat and hat again and, not bothering to take gloves, she went down the staircase. Mrs. Nash's door was closed as she passed it and she wondered if Guy Trenholm was still with her patient. She would have given much to have been present at the interview. Her thoughts veered back to Trenholm. She must see him before he left. There was something she must tell him, an idea which had come to her. Should she stay in? Miriam wavered. If she waited it would be too late to go out. Ah, she had it! Martha would give Trenholm a message for her.

Knowing that Martha usually sat in a window nook just between the pantry and the dining room, Miriam went in that direction but paused near the dining room table at sight of Betty Carter standing in the doorway leading to the sunparlor. She doubted if Betty had heard her approach, for the young girl's attention was riveted on Alan Mason, who lay asleep in one of the long wicker lounging chairs standing directly at the entrance to the dining room.

Alan's comely features were free of the haggard lines which had aged him in the past few days, and his graceful pose in the abandon of sleep resembled that of a tired boy after a day of play. Evidently his dreams were happy, for a smile trembled on his lips and he murmured softly, "Betty!"

Betty Carter's eyes were dimmed with tears and Miriam, glancing at her, read the carefully guarded secret of her heart. Alan Mason, and not his dead cousin, was the man she loved. With a swift, graceful movement Betty stooped down and kissed him on the forehead with a touch so delicate that it did not awaken the sleeping man. Then, with a gesture of utter despair, she dropped on her knees in front of a chair and buried her face in her arms.

Miriam stole softly away, her desire to see Martha forgotten in the scene she had inadvertently witnessed. It had all happened in a second of time. There had been no opportunity for her to withdraw, but Miriam felt self-reproached. Walking rapidly, head down, hands in pockets, she took no note of her direction, save that she was on a footpath leading away from Abbott's Lodge, and she honestly tried to banish Betty and Alan from her thoughts. But one idea persisted and would not down. If Betty loved Alan, why had she married Paul on Monday night?

A high wind had sprung up and Miriam had forgotten to use hatpins. The next second she was bareheaded. Her hat, a chic affair of the mushroom variety, sailed gracefully ahead of her around a curve and then another and stronger gust of wind carried it into a field on her left. With a disgusted ejaculation over her stupidity in omitting the pins, Miriam followed her hat as best she could. She had just retrieved it and slapped it vigorously on her head, regardless of the angle, when she espied a couple of cows in the corner of the field. Miriam stopped not on the order of her going and when she halted she had reached the edge of a wood. Having a good bump of locality, she recognized, after a careful glance around, the wood as the one she and Trenholm had walked through when returning from Hills Bridge.

It was growing dark and Miriam faced in the direction she judged Abbott's Lodge to be and hurried along the path. In making the next turn she paused abruptly. To her left lay the graveyard which she had remarked upon to Trenholm. Its air of desolation was emphasized by the fading light, and Miriam did not plan to linger as she had done when Trenholm was with her. But her intention to hurry past the old Mason burying plot was checked at sight of a man kneeling by a grave and digging in it with a trowel. Miriam stopped short as the man looked up. The recognition was mutual.

Corbin rose stiffly to his knees and, bending over, brushed off some dirt and dry leaves which clung to his trousers.

"How come ye here, Miss?" he demanded suspiciously.

Miriam's first impulse was to decline to answer, but Corbin had stepped back from the grave and stood almost directly in front of her, blocking the footpath.

"I am out for a walk," she replied, "and by chance came this way."

"It's lonesome like, for a lady." Corbin hitched himself a trifle closer, a beam of admiration in his watery eyes, which Miriam found more objectionable than a glare of rage.

"What are *you* doing here, Corbin?" she asked, coolly taking the situation into her hands. "What interests you in these old graves?"

Corbin shifted uneasily from one foot to the other. "Getting some ivy," he explained. "I wanted to plant some around the garage."

"So you rob a grave—"

Corbin's complexion turned an even more unhealthy color.

"Oh, the old suicide won't miss it," he said coarsely, and hastily changed the subject. "Funny, weren't it, that Mr. Paul should ha' left in his will this here graveyard to Mr. Alan, 'cause it belonged to his ancestors, and never given him nothin' else, 'cept five hundred dollars."

Miriam was not following closely Corbin's jumbled accounts of the provisions of Paul's will, which Mr. Corcoran had explained to Martha and to him at the close of the reading of the will.

"Who lies in this suicide's grave?" she asked suddenly, and the question took Corbin by surprise.

"Mr. Alan's grandfather."

"And his name?" with a persistence which surprised herself as well as Corbin.

"'Cordin' to the headstone his name was Mason, too." Talking to an extremely pretty woman was a novel sensation and Corbin was commencing to enjoy himself. "There's a saying in these parts that he stole some money when he was 'zecutor to a friend's will and killed heself when found out. The niggers buried him, as you see. Mr. Alan ain't got much call to be proud of his gran'-dad."

"But I don't think he will approve of your digging into his grave," Miriam stated quietly, "for ivy."

Corbin's lips curled back viciously over his yellow teeth. "He ain't goin' to hear of it," his voice grew low and menacing. "Not from you, anyway."

"Why not?"

He came a step nearer and his breath was unpleasantly close. "I gave the bloodstained sheet to Sheriff Trenholm," he whispered.

Miriam stared at him, open-eyed. "The bloodstained sheet!" she echoed. "What are you talking about?"

"The sheet off Mr. Paul's bed after he was murdered," with a slow, knowing wink, which sent the hot blood to her cheeks. Her color ebbed as quickly as it had come, leaving her deadly pale. "The sheriff was mighty curious to know if I had shown you where to get clean linen for the bed when you fust come. Don't worry," observing her expression and misinterpreting it. "I didn't give him no direct answer."

"What!" Corbin drew back at the force of her exclamation. "Why didn't you tell him *at once* that you showed me the linen closet?"

He leered at her. "There wasn't any call for me to give you away—then"— he supplemented.

Miriam missed the last word. Her eyes were blazing with indignation.

"And so you let Mr. Trenholm infer—"

"What he pleased—yes, Miss!"

Miriam's small hands were clenched. "You contemptible cur!" she cried, and would have added more but wrath choked her utterance.

"Here, Miss, don't you be so handy with misnamin' me," protested Corbin. "I've got feelin's like other fellows and I done ye a good turn."

"By concealing the truth!" scornfully. "You are not only a knave, Corbin, but a fool!"

"Am I?" Corbin's slow smile sent a shiver down her back in spite of her hot anger. "Come, Miss, there ain't no use o' you an' me fussin'. I'll stand yer friend, if ye'll just give me a little snow"—he came nearer and brushed her shoulder with his hand—"just a little snow."

Miriam stared at Corbin. Was the man demented? Her eyes left his face and fell on his hand as he stood stroking her coat. It was a remarkably small hand for a man, well-shaped, the long, creeping fingers stained with soil from the grave. The seal ring on his third finger caught on a button as she sprang back.

"Don't touch me!"

Corbin paid not the slightest attention to her command. His eyes aflame with desire, he stepped after Miriam and caught her hand, fawning upon her—

"You're a nurse, Miss," he whined. "Gimme a deck to-night." He saw her expression of dawning comprehension and clung to her hand more tightly than before.

Miriam wrenched her hand free. At last she understood—Corbin was a cocaine addict. For the first time she felt a twinge of fear as her glance swept the lonely countryside. Of all the demoralizing drugs, cocaine was the worst—whisky raised to its nth power was pap compared to it.

"I have none, Corbin," she said, hiding her abhorrence of the man under a brusque manner. "We nurses are no longer permitted to keep a supply of narcotics on hand."

"Doctor Roberts will let ye have a shot," eagerly. "Ye need never tell him it's for me."

"Go to him yourself."

Corbin stared at her for a long moment, his bloodshot eyes taking in her beauty appraisingly. The collar of her coat had turned back and he caught a glimpse of a gold chain. Martha had told him of rubies which she had seen around the nurse's neck.

"I'll take care o' Roberts," he said thickly. "But me an' you are goin' to come to an understandin' right now. Hand over that gold chain. Ye won't!—then, by God—"

Miriam had read the look in his eyes in time to spring aside and avoid his clutching fingers. Far more agile than her adversary, she eluded his attempt to trip her and, fear lending wings to her feet, she raced madly toward Abbott's Lodge.

Corbin's heart hammered and thumped as he strove to overtake her. He was in no physical trim and, as Miriam left the footpath and took to the fields, he sank down by the roadside, panting from his exertions. As he rested his brain cleared and he cursed aloud as he realized the folly of his act. In his mad craving for cocaine he had betrayed his precious secret to Miriam. And she would tell. Corbin ground his teeth in rage, then his face cleared. Only Miriam knew—so far. When he got up and limped toward Abbott's Lodge, his lips wrinkled in a low and vicious smile.

Finally convinced that she had outdistanced Corbin, Miriam dropped back to a walk. Considerably shaken by the fright he had given her, it took her some little time to stop looking over her shoulder to see if the caretaker was still following her. Then her thoughts switched around to Guy Trenholm and the bloodstained sheet, and her recent terror was forgotten. Had Corbin, by his evasive answers to the sheriff's question about the sheet, made Trenholm believe that she was implicated in Paul Abbott's murder? She recalled vividly his persistent questions at his bungalow that afternoon as to whether or not she had recognized Paul as the American soldier to whom her uncle had intrusted the Paltoff diamond.

Could it be that Trenholm suspected her of having recognized Paul and seized the opportunity of being alone with her patient to kill him and recover the Paltoff diamond?

The thought was torment! Miriam brushed her hair back from her forehead. She was suddenly blinded by tears, and paused in uncertainty, unable to go on. In that moment she realized what Guy Trenholm had grown to be to her. Love—had she given her love to a man unasked—unsought? Her face flamed scarlet. Had romance come into her life only to be bitter-sweet? She bowed her head in her hands and the old, familiar prayer, which had sustained her through the horrors of war and Russian revolution, again passed her lips: "God, give me strength!"

When Miriam approached the entrance of Abbott's Lodge she was once more calm and collected. As she stepped inside the house she was met by Martha.

"You are wanted upstairs in Mr. Paul's old bedroom," the housekeeper stated. "They are waitin' for ye," and giving Miriam no chance to find out who "they" were, she retreated to her kitchen, in time to meet her husband slinking in the back door.

Considerably mystified by the message, Miriam went first to her bedroom, tossed off her hat and coat, and then paused long enough to arrange her hair deftly, which had escaped from her hair net when her hat blew off. Miriam had not been in Paul's old bedroom since her interview with Trenholm the night after the murder. The door had always been closed and, never having tried to enter it, she was not aware that, by the sheriff's orders, it had been kept locked. However, she found it not only unlocked, but wide open when she reached there, and, without knocking, she stepped inside the room.

Seated near the table were Betty Carter and Guy Trenholm, and, by their attitude, she judged that they were awaiting her in growing impatience. Miriam's heart beat a trifle faster as she met Trenholm's straight gaze, but her manner was entirely natural and composed.

"You sent for me?" she asked, addressing him rather than Betty.

It was Betty who answered as Trenholm rose and placed a chair for Miriam and, from a motive which Miriam failed to guess and Trenholm himself to analyze, stood by her side, his eyes watching every play of emotion in Betty's beautiful face.

"I sent for you, Miss Ward," Betty stated, "and for Sheriff Trenholm, because I wished to see him in your presence," she faltered and grew paler. "It was before him that I flatly contradicted your statement that I was here in this room with Paul on Monday night. I wish to withdraw that denial."

The room swam around Miriam. It was the last sentence she expected from Betty. She had exonerated her and before Guy Trenholm. He would know that she had not lied. She stole a look at him. Trenholm's attention was entirely centered on Betty and his expression was difficult to decipher.

"Your motive for denying your presence here, Miss Carter?" he asked, and she winced at his tone and the formality of his address. Her woman's intuition told her that she could not sway him by feminine wiles as in the old days in Paris. He had developed from a shy country boy into a man, stern perhaps, but just, resourceful and strong. "What was your motive?" he asked again, with more emphasis, as she kept silent.

"The danger of being arrested for Paul's murder," she said, and this time it was Trenholm's turn to feel astonishment, mingled with a reluctant admiration. Betty, with characteristic courage, was taking the ground from under his feet.

"And your reason for such a fear?" he questioned swiftly.

"My marriage to Paul under such peculiar circumstances and my immediate departure, which occurred," she added, addressing Miriam, whom surprise had kept silent, "judging from your testimony, just before Paul was killed."

"Your departure just *before* he was killed is the very point which clears you of all suspicion," declared Trenholm dryly, and Betty changed color. "Come, Miss Carter, what has Paul's will to do with your sudden admission of your marriage to him?"

"Mr. Trenholm!"

"Please—no heroics!" holding up an authoritative hand. "Let us have the truth at last, Miss Carter."

Betty's eyes blazed at him wrathfully. "It is your privilege to insult a woman, I presume—one of your prequisites as sheriff of the County."

Trenholm smiled. "Put it that way, if you wish," he said, in entire good nature. "By the terms of Paul's will you inherit nothing if you marry after his death; but, as his widow, the law allows you one third of his estate, irrespective of any will," he paused—"or any marriage thereafter."

Betty rose and dropped him a curtsy, and Miriam, watching her with a critic's eye, saw no tremor in hands or lips and no evasive glance. "You make me out a very clever woman," Betty said. "I thank you."

Trenholm bowed. "There is only one flaw in your reasoning," he said. "You did not marry Paul Abbott."

Betty stared at him, astounded. "Are you mad!" she gasped. "Why, Miss Ward witnessed the marriage!"

"I beg pardon, but I was not in the room," interrupted Miriam. "Doctor Nash sent me to get a lamp and I returned just as he completed the marriage ceremony."

Betty surveyed them both scornfully. "What is this—collusion?" she demanded.

"No, just statements of facts," retorted Trenholm. "When Miss Ward returned to this room after seeing you depart, she went over to the bed and found, not Paul, but a stranger lying there."

Betty sank back in her chair. Her face was ghastly. There was no make-believe in her emotion and her half-fainting condition was genuine. With a word of explanation, Miriam bolted out of the room, to return a second later with smelling salts. Betty accepted them with a broken word of thanks.

"I don't understand," she began, glancing piteously from one to the other. "You found a strange man in Paul's bed just after I left?"

"Yes," replied Miriam, quietly. "It was a great shock and I fainted, and in that condition was chloroformed. When I revived I found Mr. Abbott lying dead in that bed."

As in a daze, Betty raised her hands and pressed them to her throbbing temples.

"You mean that some man got in this room while Miss Ward was in the hall with the lighted lamp, showing Uncle Alexander and me the way downstairs, threw Paul out of bed, and took his place?" she asked. "And being detected by Miss Ward, chloroformed her, and then murdered Paul?"

"You have described the scene very admirably," stated Trenholm, slowly, "except in one particular. The man assumed Paul's place in the bed when Miss Ward went downstairs to the door to admit you and Doctor Nash."

"Impossible!" Betty's eyes were half starting from her head. "Why, I stood near the bed—"

"Exactly where?" broke in Trenholm. "Show me."

Betty rose and walked over to the bed and paused by it. "When I came, I stopped here," she explained. "I did not move, did I, Miss Ward?" glancing appealingly at Miriam.

"No," quickly.

"And how were the curtains of the four-poster draped?" asked Trenholm.

Miriam quickly arranged them to the best of her recollection.

"Then, Miss Carter, you did not have a good view of the man in the bed?"

"But it *was* Paul," she protested. "I knew his voice."

"Voices can be imitated," Trenholm spoke slowly. "And a poor imitation would have passed muster in your state of excitement. You were expecting to find Paul there—and you were not critical."

"But I tell you I saw his face."

"How much of it?"

"His dark hair, his general contour—oh, pshaw, his beard—"

"Did you see his eyes?" asked Trenholm. "Did you lean over and kiss him?"

Betty flushed crimson, from throat to brow. "He kept his eyes closed—sick men do that"—with a defiant glance at Miriam as if challenging her to contradict her statement. "I, eh, I didn't kiss Paul because—because—" her voice died away and rose again. "He was ill and—eh—"

"And you loved another man!" Trenholm's tone cut like a whiplash, and she swayed upon her feet. "Come, confess that you consented to marry Paul because he promised you the Paltoff diamond."

Three times Betty strove to speak. "You are the devil incarnate!" she gasped. "I tell you I married Paul!" Her clenched fist struck the bedstead a sharp blow. "See, look here," and from around her neck she dragged off a gold chain which she had worn concealed underneath her gown. From it was suspended a heavy gold ring.

"You knew Paul intimately, Guy Trenholm. Do you recognize this ring?"

He took it from her hand and Miriam moved closer to his side and examined it intently. It bore only a large and beautifully carved "M" upon it. Trenholm dropped it in Miriam's hand and she was astonished at the ring's weight and its massive size.

"You know the ring's history, but Miss Ward does not," went on Betty, as Trenholm kept silent. "This ring was Paul's fetish—he was intensely superstitious. He declared that it would never leave his possession until he placed it on my finger." She drew in her breath. "Paul made that statement in your presence, Guy Trenholm, and in mine, and he placed that ring on my finger during the marriage service on Monday night."

From his leather wallet Trenholm drew a number of photographs and selected one.

"This photograph," he said, holding it so that both girls could see it, "was taken of Paul as he lay on the undertaker's couch in the room down the hall, and just before he was placed in the casket. You will see that he is still wearing his seal ring—in fact, his finger was so firmly bent to hold it upon his hand that we would have had to break the bone to take it off. His ring, Miss Carter, is buried with him."

Betty stared dumbly at him. Suddenly her strength deserted her, and before Miriam could catch her she fell in a crumpled heap at their feet.

CHAPTER XIX
WHICH?

TRENHOLM'S noiseless pacing back and forth before Betty Carter's bedroom door gave no evidence of the impatience consuming him. Miriam Ward had promised to join him the instant she was able to leave Betty. He had carried the unconscious girl to her room and then gone in search of Doctor Roberts, only to be told by Anna, who in her capacity of temporary maid was setting the dinner table, that Roberts and Alan Mason had gone for a motor ride in the former's car earlier in the afternoon.

Trenholm's restless walk drew him further and further from Betty's room and when he finally paused he found he was standing in front of the closed door where Paul Abbott's body had lain until the funeral. A hasty search in his pockets produced the key of the room and a second later he was inside it.

Trenholm took the pains to relock the door from the inside and to hang his handkerchief securely over the door knob, thereby obstructing Corbin's view of the interior of the room. The caretaker had watched the sheriff from a respectful distance and, on seeing him enter and close the door, he had stolen down the hall and, first poking out the key in the lock with a slender steel instrument, he applied his eye to the keyhole, and saw nothing. With a grunt indicative of acute disappointment, Corbin slipped up to his living quarters in pursuit of his helpmate, Martha.

When Trenholm reappeared in the hall his face was set and stern. He paused, after locking the door again and pocketing the key, to wipe tiny drops of moisture from his forehead. Were his theories entirely wrong? No, he would stake his reputation that he was right, in spite of his last discovery.

"Mr. Trenholm!" Miriam touched him on the arm and aroused him from his abstraction, an abstraction so profound that he had never heard her approach. "Miss Carter has revived and is resting quietly. I think it is safe to leave her."

"Good!" Trenholm's relief was unmistakable and sincere. "Where are you going?"

"Downstairs to see if Doctor Roberts has returned," she said, as he walked with her. She looked up at him impulsively. "Miss Carter is suffering horribly—"

"I thought you said that she was improving," halting abruptly on the landing of the staircase.

"I mean mental agony. Mr. Trenholm, can't you help her?"

"And *you* ask that?" The light in his eyes caused her to catch her breath sharply, then her heart raced on. "Come, you have never told me whom you think guilty of Paul's murder?" He led the way into the sunparlor, where Anna had lighted two of the lamps before returning to the kitchen. Trenholm adjusted the Holland shades and curtains before the windows to his satisfaction, then sat down near Miriam.

She stared at him thoughtfully before speaking. "I learned only a few hours ago of the bloodstained sheet," she said, "and that Corbin was so treacherous as to let you infer—"

He interrupted her hastily. "My inferences or deductions cleared you of any complicity in the crime," his clear, strong voice and charming smile dispelled her agonizing suspense. "I never doubted you, Miss Ward, *never*. Although the exigencies of the case may have led me to imply otherwise, I never lost faith in your integrity—your honor—your splendid courage—"

"Ahem!"

Trenholm and Miriam, who had sat enthralled drinking in his words and the message which his eyes spoke more eloquently than human lips, both looked up to find Alexander Nash standing in the doorway contemplating them.

"I drove over to see you, Trenholm, but that rascally servant of yours refused to tell me where you were to be found," explained Nash. "I then drove to Upper Marlboro and the constable finally 'allowed' you might be here. Such crass stupidity has cost me valuable time!" And Nash, the usually polished, suave clergyman as known in Washington and Toronto church circles, flung himself into a chair near Miriam, his face like a thundercloud.

"Why the excitement?" asked Trenholm, regarding him keenly.

"I have a confession to make." Nash took out his large silk handkerchief and dabbed his forehead. "No, don't go, Miss Ward—this interview holds as much interest for you as it does for the sheriff. It was in his presence that I told you that I failed to recall certain incidents of Monday night—"

"Whereby you lied," pointed out Miriam coolly, and noted with relish Nash's apoplectic complexion.

"You use a harsh term, Miss Ward," he objected. "My statement was, strictly speaking, an evasion—I did not deny that the incidents took place—simply that I did not recall them."

"Oh, come to the point!" Trenholm's tone was not complimentary, and Nash squirmed in his chair.

"Miss Carter and I were here on Monday night," he began. "And I did perform the marriage service—uniting Paul and Betty in holy wedlock."

Nash's statement did not create the excitement he had anticipated and he looked from one to the other of his companions in intense surprise.

"Did you talk with Paul?" asked Trenholm quickly.

"No—not directly. Betty told him of my presence. I stood a little distance from the bed"—he cleared his throat. "Illness is upsetting to me. I—eh—have a peculiar dread of—eh—disease. Paul made the necessary responses—after he was—eh—duly prompted."

"I see!" Trenholm was watching the agitated clergyman with disconcerting attention. "And what was your motive in denying your visit to Paul on Monday night?"

"Betty met me on my way here Tuesday afternoon and asked me not to tell of it"—Nash started up heatedly. "Why are you glaring at me in that offensive manner, Mr. Trenholm?"

"Is your first name Adam?" asked the sheriff dryly.

"No, Alexander," with indignant emphasis. "I see no occasion for levity, Mr. Trenholm. My wife is devoted to her niece and so am I. I agreed to carry out Betty's wishes, blindly it may be, and perhaps foolishly, but my motive was to protect her good name."

"Explain your meaning." Trenholm was thoroughly awake at last, and the clergyman could not complain of not creating a sensation.

"Betty received a special letter from Paul just before our departure from Toronto, telling of his illness and begging her to hurry to him," went on Nash. "He feared that he might not recover and desired her to marry him. Betty was frightfully upset, and on our approach to Baltimore asked that we leave the train there and catch the last train out for Upper Marlboro. We did so, and on reaching there I secured a Buick touring car from the local livery—" Trenholm nodded his head.

"I know that," he said. "Get on with your story."

Nash favored him with a frown. "I drove Betty out here. We left the house, as Miss Ward knows, before Paul's murder." He paused to clear his throat again. "I helped Betty into the back seat, as the curtains were up and she was more protected there, and, as the starter did not work, spent some few minutes cranking the car. Without addressing Betty again I headed the car for Washington and it was not until we were nearly at Anacostia that I discovered I was alone in the car."

"What became of Miss Carter?" demanded Trenholm, as Nash came to a dramatic pause.

"I presume she left the car when I was stooping over cranking it," explained Nash. "She had arranged the heavy laprobes so that they gave the appearance of some one seated there." Nash waited for comment from his companions, but none forthcoming, he added, a trifle pettishly, "Betty's disappearance was a great shock, but I continued on my way to Washington, wondering what I should do. Then came the news of Paul's murder and I was positively staggered. And to be greeted before I reached Abbott's Lodge with Betty's piteous plea that I say nothing of our visit here on Monday night—why, it threw me entirely off my feet. For the sake of Betty—for the fair name of my wife's family—to save them from scandal—I kept silent."

"And what has caused you to break that silence?" questioned Trenholm.

"Only to you," in alarm, "and to Miss Ward. I must ask you to pledge your word not to speak of it outside."

"And why have you told us?"

"Because you are investigating Paul's murder and I feel that you should know all the facts of the case." Nash sighed. "I learned only this morning from a reliable source that Betty spent Monday night wandering about Abbott's Lodge and in the garage. She walked to Upper Marlboro in time to catch the milk train for Washington."

"Who told you this, Doctor Nash?" asked Trenholm sternly. "I insist upon an answer."

"Well, perhaps you should know—" somewhat doubtfully. "Corbin."

Trenholm sat back and contemplated the clergyman. "Corbin," he repeated. "Thank you, Doctor Nash," as the latter rose. "How is your wife?"

"Not so well." Nash's face clouded over. "I am going to stop and see her now," he said, and with a polite bow to Miriam, he left them.

Trenholm waited until he was sure Nash had had time to reach the second floor before addressing Miriam.

"You don't admire our reverend friend?" he asked, noting with secret amusement her wrathful expression.

"I think he is horrid!" she ejaculated. "So—so slimy. And Mrs. Nash is so straightforward and absolutely sincere." Hastily she changed the subject. "How did that last code message read?"

Trenholm looked carefully around before answering her, to be sure they were alone, then approaching close to her side, whispered it in her ear.

"'Watch thirteenth letter. Suicides grave.'"

"It sounds like gibberish," she murmured. "Do you still think it refers to the thirteenth letter of the alphabet?"

"I do," firmly. "And quite appropriately so," he went on slowly, "when it commences such words as morphine, murder, madness—"

"And Mason," she completed, quietly. "But, Mr. Trenholm, it's a poor rule that doesn't work both ways—"

"What do you mean?" as she paused.

"Counting the alphabet from A to M is thirteen," she said. "But counting from M to A the thirteenth letter is *A*." She looked at him queerly. "*Alexander Nash*."

"Why not Alan Mason—counting *both* ways his initials make the number thirteen?" Trenholm stuffed his hands into his pockets and gazed at her tall, shapely figure, her clear, olive skin, and her great beautiful eyes, and was conscious of an accelerated pulse. He came a step closer. "I have learned that Alan was on the troopship from Vladivostok with his cousin Paul."

She started and stared at him aghast. "I can't believe Mr. Mason had a hand in the murder," she declared vehemently. "Call it instinct—or what you will—I believe absolutely that Mr. Abbott's murder was planned and carried out by Boris Zybinn, and I cannot forget that Alexander Nash was Zybinn's neighbor in Toronto. Tell me," she came closer to his side, "has Doctor Nash a parish in Washington?"

"No—nor in Toronto." Trenholm stroked his chin reflectively. "I understand that he was a man of considerable means before he married Representative Carter's daughter—and that in spite of the difference in their ages, it was a love match, pure and simple. I think Paul told me that Doctor Nash had retired from the ministry."

"O-o-h!" Miriam's exclamation was long-drawn out and Trenholm stared. She gave him no opportunity to question her further. "To go back to the coded message," she began, "have you thought the words 'suicides grave' have any connection with the Mason plot out yonder and the poor suicide— that makes the thirteenth grave—as you pointed out the other day, in that neglected family cemetery?"

Trenholm looked at her keenly. "Time will show," he replied, and wondered at her disappointment. "Why do you ask?"

"I walked by the graveyard just now," she said hurriedly, "and was amazed to see—"

"Excuse me, Miss—Ma'am"—Martha's complaining voice caused Miriam to jump—startled by the woman's proximity. "Dinner will be ready in a minute. I've just telled the folks upstairs, and thought mebbe you'd like to know. There's a couple o' boys outside inquirin' for ye, Sheriff," and, her message delivered, Martha took herself off.

Trenholm caught up with her before she reached the kitchen, and drew her to one side.

"Martha!" His low stern voice sent a shiver down the woman's back, and the pressure of his hand on her arm tightened. "When did this letter reach Mr. Paul?" and he held before her the thirteenth letter. "No lies, now. I want the truth."

"Yes, sir," Martha's quavering tones did not belie her feelings. "Please, sir, that there letter with them queer stamps come the morning Mr. Paul was killed, sir."

"No go, Martha," Trenholm shook her slightly. "The postmark shows this letter should have reached Upper Marlboro last week."

"I ain't sayin' it didn't," she whined. "But by mistake it was put in Anna's father's box by the carrier; an' havin' sickness in the family, Anna only brought it up on Monday mornin'. I took it from her, sir, and went right up to the room where Mr. Paul was talkin' to Mr. Alan—an' laid it on the table."

"Mr. Alan!" Trenholm strove to keep his voice lowered. "Was he here then?"

"Yes, sir. Mr. Paul sent for him," she looked up craftily. "He stayed 'round most of the day until 'bout time the doctor was to come, and then he cleared out." She raised herself on tiptoe and whispered as he bent down to hear her better. "Corbin wa'n't here then. He'd kill me if he knew I was keepin' anythin' from him. But Mr. Alan," her voice held unexpected, unmistakable pathos, "years back, he beat Corbin for mishandlin' me, and I ain't never forgot how good he was."

"Hush!" Trenholm took out his handkerchief and handed it to her. "Dry your eyes, Martha; and say nothing about Mr. Alan or this letter"—returning it to his pocket. "Remember I trust you."

Martha drew a long, long breath. Trenholm was treating her like a human being. Gratitude, mingled with a return of self-respect, caused her to raise his hand to her lips, then, in frantic bashfulness, she slipped back into the dining room, upsetting Anna in her hurried entrance.

Trenholm paused in deep thought, then, going through the side door, joined the three deputies who were anxiously awaiting him. His concise directions were listened to with the respect which Trenholm inspired among those who worked with and for him.

"You understand," he said finally, and the men nodded as they stood grouped about him. "Riley, go to the telegraph office and await the answers to the messages I have sent and bring them to me. Do not permit them to telephone any message to me; there is too much danger of 'listening in.' Now, be off," and Trenholm again entered Abbott's Lodge, but by the front door.

Trenholm's entrance went unnoticed by Doctor Roberts and Alan Mason, who were chatting with Miriam, while Alexander Nash stood moodily contemplating the blazing logs on the hearth at the further end of the living room, deaf alike to his companions and Anna's announcement that dinner was served.

With old-fashioned courtesy, Roberts offered his arm to Miriam, then paused abruptly as footsteps on the staircase caused him to glance upward.

"God bless my soul!" he ejaculated in complete surprise.

Coming down the staircase, with the assistance of a flurried Somers, was Mrs. Nash. She had donned a pretty negligée, and the excitement and her exertions combined had brought the color to her face. Miriam hastened to Somers' assistance and Roberts was immediately behind her.

"This is most imprudent, Mrs. Nash!" he exclaimed sternly. "In your condition—"

"Poof!" Mrs. Nash snapped her fingers. "I am getting on famously. Don't be pessimistic, Doctor; instead, you should congratulate me upon my recovery. Thank you, my dear," as Miriam helped her toward the dining room. "Come here, Alexander, and give me your arm."

At sound of her voice, the clergyman wheeled around and stepped backward with such suddenness that he walked on the fire tongs and fender.

"Dora—here! Have you taken leave of your senses?" he demanded.

"I seem the only one to have retained my senses," she retorted tartly. "Miss Ward, you were always assuring me I was not very ill, but judging from

Doctor Roberts' conduct and my husband's, they must have thought me at the point of death."

Nash collected his scattered wits and came forward. "I suppose you will have your way, though the skies fall," he said resignedly. "But I should have thought, my dear, that poor Zybinn's sudden death through imprudent neglect of his health would have warned you to be careful."

What rejoinder Mrs. Nash made was lost by Trenholm, who had stood out of sight behind the grandfather clock watching the scene. He waited until, judging from the sounds that came from the other room, they were seated around the dinner table, and then, taking care to make no noise, he ran lightly up the staircase and darted into Mrs. Nash's bedroom.

Before going to her supper, Somers had aired the room and remade the bed, and Trenholm's electric torch showed everything in order. First convincing himself that he was the only person in the bedroom, he went over to the wall and taking from his pocket the pen and ink drawing which he had carried away almost under Mrs. Nash's nose, he hung it back in its place.

Trenholm laid down his torch on a convenient chair and drew out the thirteenth letter. He had inserted a little paste under the flap before leaving his bungalow, and to all intents and purposes the envelope looked as if it never had been opened. Holding it in his hand, he scanned the bedroom eagerly and spied a dustpan and brush which Somers had carelessly forgotten and left standing by the bureau. Trenholm slipped over to it and laid the envelope on the small pile of trash in the pan. When he had arranged it to his liking, the envelope looked as if it had been brushed up with the rest of the trash, but the Canadian stamps were plainly in view.

Trenholm stood up and, taking his torch with him, tiptoed to the hall door which he had left open as he had found it. A glance outside showed that the hall was empty. Looking about the bedroom, Trenholm noticed a screen which Somers had brought into the bedroom and stood between Mrs. Nash and an open window. It would make an excellent hiding place. Like a flash he was behind it. From where he crouched, he had an excellent view of the open door and the entire bedroom. Trenholm drew a long breath—the stage was set, and he had staked all on the fall of the dice!

Half an hour passed and he was commencing to worry when a light footfall came down the hall and he heard Betty Carter exclaim at sight of the darkened room.

"Somers!" she called, very softly. Getting no reply, she peered into the room and then very cautiously came inside it. A startled exclamation, quickly suppressed, escaped her at sight of the empty bed, and she drew back and glanced hastily over her shoulder. Gathering courage from the continued stillness, she went over to the bureau and fumbled in one of the drawers. Something fell from her hand—from Trenholm's position he could not see what, and he dared not move—and she struck a match. Shielding it in her hand, she stooped over. She remained so long in that position that Trenholm grew alarmed; then, with a swiftness and stealth which left him breathless, she was gone.

Had Betty taken the thirteenth letter? Trenholm was on edge, but, before he dared venture out, another figure stood in the doorway, and by the light from the hall lamp, he recognized Miriam. Without hesitation she went at once to the bureau and opening the second drawer took out one of Mrs. Nash's scarfs. Would she see the envelope and, thinking it had accidentally fallen in the dustpan, pick it up? Or was it not there for her to pick up? Trenholm heaved a sigh of thankfulness when Miriam turned and went into the hall.

A stealthy step inside the bedroom a few seconds later caused Trenholm again to draw back into the shelter of the screen in time to miss being seen by Corbin. The caretaker had advanced only a few paces when a hand was laid on his shoulder and he was jerked back.

"*Sacré Dieu!* What do you in my mistress' bedroom, *cochon?*" hissed Pierre in his ear. What answer the terrified man would have made was checked by Alexander Nash's voice in the hall.

"Pierre, bring the car around!" Nash failed to see the two men, chauffeur and caretaker, steal out of his wife's doorway, for he turned at the moment to address Alan Mason—only to find that the young man had disappeared. Nash hesitated for a fraction of a second, then tiptoed down the hall.

Trenholm's sensitive ears caught the creak of a floor board, and the faint "seep—seep" of something being dragged across the floor. A flood of light from an electric torch half blinded him, accustomed to the almost total darkness of the room, and he rubbed his eyes to clear his vision, just as the light was focused full upon the dustpan. The thirteenth letter stood out in bold relief. The light was dimmed instantly and again Trenholm caught the sound of something creeping across the floor.

The light flared up again with unexpected swiftness and Trenholm saw a shapeless figure, its head and shoulders enveloped in some black garment, squatting over the dustpan. The torch lay at rest by it, and Trenholm had a glimpse of long, slender fingers holding the letter as he crept from behind the screen and as noiseless as the shadows about him, reached the kneeling figure. The stamped envelope was held in one hand and in the other was a perforation gauge—

With lightning swiftness Trenholm snapped the handcuffs on the two upraised wrists. With a sweep of his arm, he drew back the black, shroudlike garment, as he cried:

"In the name of the law I arrest you for the murder of Paul Abbott"— Trenholm's voice died away at sight of the distorted, ghastly face confronting him, then rose in horror—"Doctor Roberts."

CHAPTER XX
THE RULING PASSION

BETTY CARTER, too unhappy to keep to her room, where she had found bed intolerable after recovering from her faint, was the first to hear Roberts' frantic cries for mercy as Trenholm got him upon his feet and half dragged, half lifted his prisoner into a chair. She stood aghast in the doorway of Mrs. Nash's bedroom until pushed further inside by Alan Mason and Doctor Nash, who had paused to pick up a lighted lamp and carried it with him. Mrs. Nash, leaning heavily on Miriam's arm, was likewise not slow in reaching her room, while Martha was only restrained from racing upstairs also by a terrified Anna, whose detaining clutch she could not loosen.

"Good God!" Alan dashed to Trenholm's side as Roberts, his paroxysm over, sank weakly back in his chair and covered his face with his manacled hands. "What is the meaning of this, Guy?"

"Doctor Roberts murdered Paul Abbott," stated Trenholm, and his announcement created a profound sensation.

Mrs. Nash dropped into the nearest seat, for once bereft of speech, while Alan, his face transfigured, stumbled over to Betty, and kneeling, pressed her hand to his lips.

"Betty, my darling!" he exclaimed incoherently. "I knew that you were here on Monday night, and then you denied your visit. Corbin told me that you had bribed him into giving up your bloodstained scarf. God forgive me! I was afraid that you had killed Paul."

"Do not reproach yourself too much," she said, and her soft, clear voice held its old accustomed thrill. Unmindful of the presence of the others, she drew him to his feet and his arms encircled her. "I did you a greater wrong, Alan, when I married Paul, while my heart was given to you."

"But you did not marry Paul—you married me," declared Alan, and but for his supporting arm Betty would have fallen.

"You—she married you!" Mrs. Nash was getting her fill of excitement. With eyes half starting from her head, she gazed at her niece and Alan. "You—Alan"—while her husband feebly echoed her words.

"Yes"—facing their concentrated regard with head thrown back, his face alight with hope and love, Alan's voice rang out clearly. "Paul sent for me and I spent Monday morning with him. Just before I left came your telegram, Betty, saying that you and Nash were on your way here and that you would marry him. It was a frightful shock, and for hours I wandered about the countryside, keeping out of people's way. I determined to see Paul again and tell him of my passionate love for you, Betty—" he sighed. "I must have been a bit mad—"

Betty pressed his hand. "Go on," she begged; "don't stop."

"I reached here after midnight and knocked on the side door, but could not arouse Corbin," continued Alan. "Paul and I had often entered the house in the old days when he had forgotten his doorkey, by climbing up to the veranda roof and entering a window of his room. As I reached his window, which was conveniently open, I heard the front door bell ring loudly. I judged it was Betty arriving with Doctor Nash and, pausing to take off my muddy shoes and overcoat, I left them outside on the roof, and then dropped inside the bedroom and rushed over to speak to Paul. The bed was empty."

"Great heavens!" Miriam stared, astounded, at Alan. "Where was Mr. Abbott?"

"I don't know," admitted Alan. "At the time I supposed he was out in the hall, as I could hear voices. When they came closer I climbed into the empty bed, to avoid being seen, and pulled the bedclothes up over me. I couldn't face Betty and Paul in their, what I supposed to be, hour of happiness. I was horrified when Betty and Nash came directly into the bedroom, and I suddenly realized that they took me for Paul."

"Were you wearing a false beard?" asked Trenholm.

"No, not a false one. I had let my beard grow for the past two weeks," explained Alan, "and shaved it off on Tuesday morning. To go back to the scene in the bedroom—the lamp had gone out, and except for the firelight the room was dark, and I prayed that Betty would leave without recognizing me. Before I could collect my senses, Doctor Nash read the marriage service—"

"And you made the responses?"

"Yes; the doctor prompted me." Alan flushed hotly, then paled. "I think I was mad that night. My voice is like Paul's."

"It was your greatest point of resemblance," commented Trenholm, "and the recollection of it finally gave me the key to the situation."

Alan turned to Miriam and spoke with honest contrition. "I didn't know that Paul had a nurse," he said. "You weren't here in the morning. I was still lying in Paul's bed, trying dazedly to plan something—anything—when I heard some one return and walk swiftly to the bed. I heard your outcry and the sound of your fall, and," in shame-faced honesty, "I bolted out of the window, gathered up my hat, coat and shoes, and fled."

"Just a moment," broke in Trenholm. "How about the ring you gave Miss Carter?"

Alan eyed him in surprise. "Oh, the ring?" he echoed. "Paul gave it to me Monday morning—that was why I happened to have it about me."

"And why did Paul give you a ring which he valued with almost superstitious fervor?" inquired Trenholm.

"It wasn't his original ring, but an exact replica which, Paul told me on Monday, he had had made for me. The original ring was a gold coin of the First century of the Christian era and belonged to my grandfather, another Alan Mason—"

"The suicide?"

Alan winced slightly as he bowed. "I don't know Paul's motive in having the ring copied for me—he often did freakish, unaccountable things."

His remarks were checked by an exclamation from Roberts, who had regained some semblance of self-control while listening to Alan.

"There was no accounting for what Paul would do," he stated, and all eyes turned to him, partly in curiosity, but more in unconcealed horror. "I may as well make my confession now as later," he sighed. "After I left Abbott's Lodge I motored to Upper Marlboro, deciding, as it was such a bad night, that I would remain at the hotel. It was before midnight when Corbin came in and told me that a letter had come that day from Canada from Zybinn and that he had taken it, with other papers, to the room Paul used as a sitting room. I gave Corbin his customary bribe—"

"Cocaine," interposed Miriam quickly, and Roberts nodded.

"I took Corbin's key to the front door," he went on, speaking with more of an effort, "and came back to find the letter which," turning with a scowl to Trenholm, "with your infernal astuteness, you divined bore a stamp code. You planted that letter and this trap—"

"I did," admitted Trenholm quietly. "I realized that the thirteenth letter had not been read either by Paul or the person for whom the code was intended. Knowing that attempts had been made to steal something from this room, I judged that the letter had been lost here, and so"—with a quiet smile at Mrs. Nash—"I arranged to have the room vacated for an hour or two. I knew whoever would attempt to steal that letter had killed Paul."

"But why?" demanded Doctor Nash.

"Because the stamp code tells where Paul had secreted the Paltoff diamond."

"It does!" Roberts was on his feet; his features distorted. "Good God! to think that I failed by so short a margin."

"Sit down!" directed Trenholm, with a significant pressure on the physician's shoulder. "What did you do, Roberts, when you reached Abbott's Lodge on Monday night?"

"I stole softly up here." Roberts moistened his parched lips. "I found the letter which Corbin had placed on the table and took up the nut pick, intending to open the envelope, take out the letter and leave it, and study the stamp code at my leisure at the hotel. A noise at my elbow caused me to glance around—Paul was standing at my side."

"Well—what next?" prompted Trenholm, as Roberts ceased speaking.

"My face must have betrayed me," he continued, a second later. "Paul's unexpected appearance shocked me out of my self-control. He turned, I suppose to call for help, and I drove the nut pick into his back."

There was a pause which none cared to break. Roberts wiped some perspiration from his forehead and then spoke more rapidly.

"I stood gazing down at the dead man, for I had turned out the lamp which I had lighted only a second before, and waited in the dark, my brain whirling. Paul had left the door partly open and I not only heard but saw Betty and Nash and Miss Ward enter Paul's bedroom. Every instant I expected to hear an outcry when they discovered Paul was not in the bed. The suspense was something frightful"—his voice shook, and he steadied it with an effort. "Peering out from behind the door I saw Nash and Betty leave, and Miss Ward return to Paul's bedroom. There followed a slight cry, a heavy fall, and then silence. I waited for a second or two, then crept across the hall and into the bedroom. Miss Ward was lying in a faint on the floor, and Paul's bed was empty."

"So, fearing she would revive too soon, you chloroformed her and carried Paul's dead body into the room and put it into his bed," completed Trenholm, as Roberts broke down, unable to go on. "How did you lose the letter?"

"I don't know—it is the one confused incident of the night," replied Roberts, after some hesitation. "The letter must have flown out of my hand as I struck at Paul." Roberts sighed heavily. "It happened that Paul fell on some soiled sheets which Martha had thrown on the floor, intending to take away the next morning. I used the sheets and a woman's scarf to staunch the flow of blood and gave them, with my driving gloves, which I had not removed, to Corbin to destroy. There was nothing to indicate that Paul had been in this bedroom, nothing to link me with the crime." Roberts sighed again. "Then

- 148 -

an overwhelming terror and an unspeakable horror of what I had done drove me out of the house and I did not come again into this bedroom to make a search for the letter. The next morning Alan and Trenholm and the coroner gave me no time alone, and then came Mrs. Nash and she was put in here—and with her awake in the daytime and Miss Ward on duty at night"—Roberts' gesture was eloquent as he looked at Trenholm. "Well, you beat me. But I'd like to know where you found the letter and how you discovered the code."

"Miss Ward did both," replied Trenholm as they looked at him. "She found the letter in that chair," pointing to it, "tucked under the upholstery and the seat cushion where it evidently had fallen; and she suspected that a code was concealed in the peculiar use of five one-cent Canadian stamps, in place of the regular three-cent postage, on thirteen letters. We deciphered the code—and this message:—"

"Well?" questioned Roberts eagerly, as he paused. "What?"

"'Watch thirteenth letter suicides grave,'" repeated Trenholm, and his listeners gazed at him blankly. Turning abruptly to Betty, he addressed her. "Did you take some photographs of this house a little while ago, and one of this room?"

"Why, yes," she exclaimed. "Just before I went to Canada, and Mr. Zybinn developed the negatives for me. He was a paralytic, and while unable to walk, dabbled in photography. He had some enlargements made of my kodak films."

"And one of this room?" quickly.

"Yes. He said it was a remarkably good interior and made me describe all the objects in it—"

"Especially this"—going over to the wall, Trenholm took down a picture and held it in plain view. He stopped as the constable and Riley came into the bedroom, the latter with a sheaf of telegrams in his hand. "Ah, Constable, you are just in time—this picture was made by Paul's mother, who was an artist of some ability. She modeled it after those quaint Swiss paintings of a cemetery with a church in the background, in which a *real* clock was put in the tower. In this picture of the Masons' neglected burying ground, Mrs. Abbott etched in the background a church tower and *placed in the tower this antique watch.*"

Trenholm turned the picture around and pointed to a watch, a tiny affair, which was firmly held in the canvas by a clever contrivance. He drew out the watch with a careful hand, the others watching him breathlessly.

"The first word of the code is 'watch.' Here it is," Trenholm held up the antique watch. "The next two words, 'thirteenth letter,' which is 'M', you will find is the initial engraved on the back of the watch; and the last two words, 'suicide's grave,' exemplified by this picture of Colonel Mason's grave." Trenholm turned to Betty and asked: "Did you not tell Zybinn that you chanced to see Paul remove the works from this watch?"

"Yes," she admitted. "Zybinn asked me if the watch was too old to keep accurate time and I told him Paul had taken it apart."

"So that was it," and Trenholm nodded. "Paul removed the works from the watch because he evidently judged it to be an admirable hiding place for—"

"The Paltoff diamond!" shouted Roberts.

For answer Trenholm opened the watch. Inside the round hollow lay a wad of cotton—and on top of it the lost jewel.

They gathered about the table, even Roberts, forgetful for a brief second that he was handcuffed, and gazed at the beautiful gem, dazzled by its luster and purity.

Trenholm was the first to speak. "Paul knew little rest after the Paltoff diamond was intrusted to his care. He was constantly haunted by a morbid fear of losing it or of being robbed of it, so that he could never be induced to exhibit it."

"He showed it to Betty and to me," declared Mrs. Nash, breaking her long silence. "And swore us to absolute secrecy. I greatly feared," she added, "that Betty was in some way mixed up in the tragedy and my husband's extraordinary denial of their presence here on Monday, when Pierre had brought me Betty's telegram to Paul, fed my imagination—and—and—I dropped that note to you, Mr. Trenholm, and—" not meeting her husband's reproachful glance, but looking instead at Miriam—"I took surreptitious doses of phenacetin and accidentally overdid it and nearly killed myself, but," with a return of her old arrogant air, "I was determined to find out what was going on in this house, whatever the consequences."

"I see," Trenholm concealed a smile, and then grew grave. "The usual ill-luck, apparently inseparable from the possession of great diamonds, has overtaken Paul," he said sorrowfully. "He remained true to his trust and never parted with the jewel. Miss Ward," with an abruptness which startled her from her study of Roberts, whose eyes had never left the diamond, "your uncle, M. Paltoff, gave the gem to Paul—they are both dead—what do you wish done with it?"

She could not prevent a shudder. "I cannot take it," she protested. "Can you not turn it over to the Department of State and let the Government decide as to its disposition?"

"An excellent suggestion." Trenholm, after replacing the diamond in its hiding place, secreted the watch carefully in an inside pocket. "Stand back, Roberts," as the physician made an effort to wrench it from him. "You will go with the constable and Riley, but first," his voice deepened, "how was it that you, supposedly a reputable physician and a man of honor, joined Zybinn in his endeavor to steal the Paltoff diamond?"

Roberts turned sullenly, the veneer gone; and a criminal, crafty and sinister-eyed, faced them.

"I am a drug addict," he admitted. "I became so two years ago after a nervous breakdown. I was ship's surgeon on the transport with Paul. He sent for me and I removed the diamond from the wound in his leg. I was straight then. My practice had fallen off; I was, in fact, a ruined man when, on a visit to Doctor Nash, I met Zybinn. He wormed Paul's secret out of me, and promised, if I would steal the jewel, to give me half the value of the diamond. I knew he had money, for he had deposited a large fortune in a bank in Toronto before fleeing from Russia after a quarrel with Lenin. Zybinn pointed out that the diamond was too celebrated to be negotiable in the usual channels, and that, cut into smaller stones, it would lose most of its value, and so I agreed to his terms."

"And why the stamp code?" asked Trenholm, as Roberts came to an abrupt halt.

"Doctor Nash had employed me to travel with Paul and keep him under observation, and it was thought wiser for Zybinn not to communicate directly with me," Roberts turned to Miriam. "A glass of water, please." Riley got it for him, before Miriam could move, from the pitcher placed for Mrs. Nash's use on the bedstand.

Roberts looked over at Betty, a malignant grin distorting his face.

"Zybinn used you as a cat's paw," he said. "Through you he gained an intimate knowledge of Paul's habits, his mode of life, and, using his remarkable powers of deduction, twice located the hiding place of the diamond—in each instance too late, for Paul's capricious habits, his secretiveness, yes," with grudging admiration, "his cleverness balked us. And so did you," wheeling on Mrs. Nash with a suddenness which made her jump. "I tried to secure the thirteenth letter on Tuesday night, but Martha detected me, and last night you pulled off my disguise."

"Why did you risk discovery?" asked Mrs. Nash. "Why not have telegraphed to Zybinn for the message on his last letter?"

"I telephoned from Washington on Tuesday and was told he had died from apoplexy on Monday afternoon—his third stroke," added Roberts. "That message on his letter to Paul was Zybinn's last word to me. He thought I was still here at Abbott's Lodge."

"Just a moment," broke in Trenholm. "Why did Zybinn use the words 'thirteenth letter' to designate the initial 'M' on the back of the watch?"

"Because in devising our code we failed to make provision for indicating an initial, expecting never to use one." Roberts chafed one cold hand over the other. "Had I decoded Zybinn's last message, I'd have gotten his meaning, however, for that little sketch is the only painting by Paul's mother on the premises and always cherished by her son. He invariably spoke of the sketch as 'The Suicide's Grave.'"

"I told Zybinn that," admitted Betty. "Great heavens! how I played into his hands—"

"Just so!" agreed Roberts with sneering emphasis. He straightened up, swayed slightly and recovered his balance with an effort. "Come," addressing Trenholm, "I can stand no more."

The constable was by his side and Riley at his heels instantly. "We'll take him to Upper Marlboro, sir," the former stated, and at a nod from Trenholm, Roberts, with eyes averted from his former friends, left the room, the black shroudlike cloth still thrown about his shoulders—typical in its vague outlines of the shadowed and complex nature of the man.

Mrs. Nash's overcharged feelings found relief in tears. "There," she exclaimed, as her distracted husband held a glass of water and Miriam the smelling salts. "I'll be myself in a minute. Betty, come and tell me why you remained here, instead of returning to Washington with your uncle, and why you lied about your visit to Paul."

Betty cleared her throat. "You were partly responsible—"

"I?" her aunt regarded her in astonishment.

"Yes. After leaving the house I remembered my promise to Uncle Alexander to telephone you why we were detained, and while he was cranking the car, I jumped out and rang the bell. No one came and I waited and rang again. Looking around I saw that Uncle had driven off. I tried to overtake him and failed, so spent the night here in Paul's garage, the door being unlocked. Martha found me there in the morning and gave me some breakfast. She told me Paul had been murdered. It was a frightful shock!" Betty drew in her breath. "And I lost my head and ran away; and, to make bad matters worse, denied my visit here." She turned impulsively to Alan.

"You will never know the suffering I have endured since Monday," she said, and her voice quivered with emotion. She read his expression, and a look of hope, of joy, flashed up in her face. "Am I forgiven?"

Alan's arms were around her, his lips against hers. "You are loved," he whispered. "Does not that cover all?" and he led her from the room.

Martha intercepted Miriam as she was on her way to her own room an hour later.

"He's waiting downstairs," she said, pointing in the direction of the living room.

"He?—Who?"

"Mr. Trenholm." And Martha who, since Corbin's arrest for complicity in Paul's murder and for having narcotics concealed in his cache in the suicide's grave, had kept carefully hidden in the kitchen closet, stole softly to bed.

Trenholm dropped the paper he was reading as Miriam paused in front of him, and sprang to his feet.

"I hoped that you would come," he said. "Betty and Alan are in the sunparlor. In our talk they have cleared up the last threads of the mystery. It seems that Betty's telegram to Paul was telephoned out from Upper Marlboro and Alan wrote it down on a slip of paper and gave it to him. It was to secure that paper, Betty thinking it a regular telegraph blank, that they both tried to search this house and my bungalow."

"Mr. Abbott had a paper in his hand when he told me that Miss Carter would be here," broke in Miriam.

"Ah, then he must have carried it with him into the sitting room, and dropped it on the way there," replied Trenholm. "Pierre found it and took it to Mrs. Nash."

A ghost of a smile hovered about Miriam's lips. "I cannot help but like Mrs. Nash," she confessed, then changed the subject swiftly. "What took Mr. Abbott into the sitting room when I went downstairs to admit Miss Carter and Doctor Nash?"

Trenholm shook his head. "We will never know, but I imagine it was some sixth sense which warned him of danger to the diamond—the gem seemed to exert a remarkable influence over him. Poor Paul!" Trenholm sighed. "His extraordinary will-power triumphed over physical disability and gave him strength to reach the sitting room."

Miriam's eyes filled with tears. "I cannot shake off a sense of responsibility for the tragedy—"

"Nonsense!" Trenholm spoke with the vehemence characteristic of him. "Never think that."

Miriam's smile did not dispel the shadow which saddened her expression.

"It is good-by, Mr. Trenholm," she said, holding out her hand. "I leave for Washington early to-morrow."

Trenholm's hand closed over hers with a pressure that hurt.

"Good-by," he repeated mechanically. "No, I can't let you go out of my life; for you have become all in all to me." As he met the gaze of her lovely eyes, his set speech, which he had rehearsed again and again while waiting to see her, flew out of his mind.

"Miriam, I have only love to offer—" His clear voice faltered. For a second they gazed steadfastly at each other, and the old, old story which never grows old was told again as Trenholm clasped Miriam to his heart and her lips met his in unconditional surrender.

THE END